Other titles by the author

If Frogs Could Fly

written under the pseudonym

E.B. Mendel

the Help of Angels

a historical novel with an unearthly twist

H. J. Zeger

Sunbridge Books

Deerfield Beach Florida

Published by Sunbridge Books

sunbridgebooks@gmail.com

Library of Congress

ISBN: 9798359159234

Book design by H.J. Zeger

Front cover illustration from an original painting by Justin Love

Photograph on back cover under copyright

Book cover designed by E Book Launch

Printed in the U.S.A.

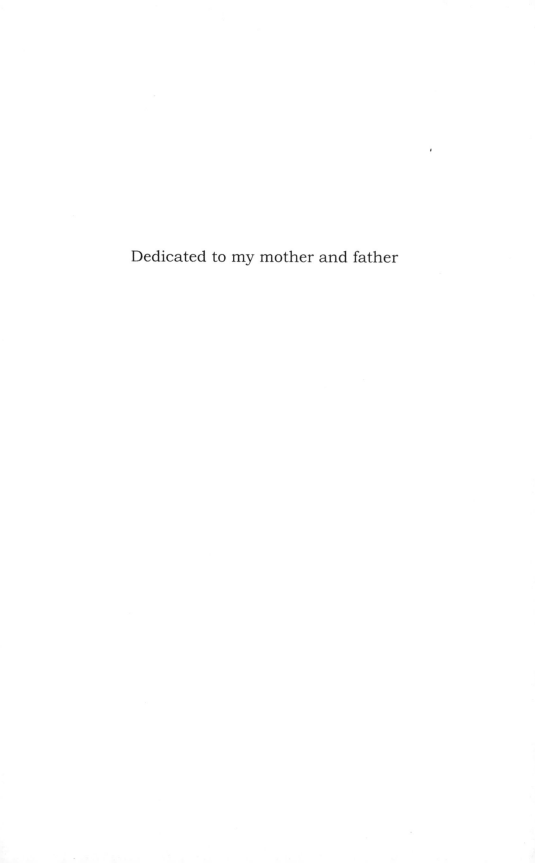

Dedicated to my mother and father

The Help of Angels

1

Beregszász, Hungary

January 1933

Hanni Weiss placed two Sabbath candles on a credenza, and she lit them with a wooden match. Her three daughters, Pearl, Zipporah, Raisel and youngest son, Herschel, watched while their mother placed her hands over her eyes and recited a Hebrew blessing.

"Blessed art Thou, O Lord our God, King of the Universe, who sanctified us by Thy laws and commanded us to kindle the Sabbath lights."

Hanni opened her eyes and waved her hands above the flames, drawing the devout illumination inward. She donned a white apron and returned to the kitchen with her older daughters, who helped their mother prepare the Sabbath evening meal. Raisel and Herschel sang while they set the dining room table: "Hava nagila, hava nagila, hava nagila ve-nismeḥa. Let's sing, let's sing, let's sing and be happy."

* * *

After Friday evening services, Mendel Weiss and his four older sons, Ignatz, Arnon, Mordecai, and Benjamin, departed the great synagogue of Beregszász, and they happily walked home together. A crescent moon and stars provided them light as they passed the darkened shops on Main Street. Their route took them across a bridge above a river, through a tree-filled park, and then onto a cobblestone road where they lived. Bereg Street. Benjamin opened an iron gate for his father and brothers; they walked through and approached the front door. Each of them touched the mezuzah on the doorpost before entering the three-story white stucco house.

On his way to wash his hands, Benjamin stopped to observe the brightly glowing Sabbath candles on the credenza. He remained there while his father and brothers washed their hands.

"Go wash, Ben," his father said, before sitting at the head of the dining room table.

"Oh, I will, Papa."

Ben withdrew his eyes from the light, and he quickly proceeded to clean his hands at the washing area. He sat while Mendel's oldest son, Ignatz, lifted a decorative cloth that covered a sweet-smelling braided bread called challah; Hanni had baked it specially for the Sabbath. The tall, dark-haired Ignatz recited the blessing over the bread.

"Praised be Thou, O Lord our God, King of the Universe, who brings forth bread from the earth."

"Amen," everyone at the table responded.

Ignatz tasted a small piece of the challah, then cut ten slices from the loaf before it was passed around the table. Hanni and her three daughters served steaming bowls of chicken soup. Parsley, sliced carrot, and long thin egg noodles floated on top. The women sat.

* * *

After Ben swallowed his last bite of chicken, he savored the apple pie Zipporah had baked. His mother poured him a glass of sweet red wine; he drank, and it made him drowsy. The boy yawned while gazing at the flickering candle flames once more. Mendel proudly glanced over at his thirteen-year-old son. The next morning Ben would have his bar mitzvah ceremony in the synagogue.

"Why don't you go to sleep, Benjamin?" his mother said. "You have a long day tomorrow."

"I will, Mama."

The thirteen-year-old got up from the table, and he washed his silverware, glass, and plate in the kitchen. He came out to the dining room again, tousled little Herschel's hair, and then bid everyone a good night. He went upstairs, brushed his teeth, undressed, and then climbed into a bed he shared with his older brother, Mordecai. A strong wind knocked the window shutters against the side of the house as Ben closed a book and extinguished a kerosene lamp by the bed. His eyes grew weary. He settled onto his pillow and fell into a deep slumber. The rest of the family retired soon afterward.

Downstairs, the remaining candlelight formed specter-like images upon the dining room walls and ceiling. Shadowy faces and distorted arms, hands, and legs swayed in a macabre-like Sabbath dance. A powerful gust of wind blew in through the dining room window, knocking over a candlestick and igniting the tablecloth. It rapidly caught the curtains on fire. The blaze climbed the dry wood staircase to the second-floor bedroom, then up to the attic. Ben felt the heat singe his ears, nose, and eyelids. His name was shouted beyond the smoky sleep.

"Benjamin! The house is on fire!"

Someone shook Ben's arm, and he quickly sat up and opened his eyes. There was no fire or smoke in the pitch-black bedroom in the attic. The wind had stopped blowing and the window shutters had become still.

"What's the matter, Ben?" Mordecai asked, "Who were you just talking to?"

"Nobody, I must have been dreaming. Go back to sleep."

2

Benjamin woke up in the early morning; the frightening nightmare vividly replayed in his mind. He got out of bed and went down to the outhouse behind the barn. After he relieved himself, he washed his hands and face from a water spigot in the yard. Ben returned to the bedroom and anxiously dressed for his bar mitzvah, donning a brand-new suit, necktie, and a pair of glossy black shoes Mr. Jacob Katz, the shoemaker had made for the occasion. Ben stood four feet ten inches but possessed a fit and limber body. He loved sports. Especially soccer. An unusual birthmark on the outer side of his left nostril drew attention to a long and well-formed nose. Prominent cheek bones, large ears, and thin gentle lips accentuated his intense yet congenial face. Ben looked in the mirror and brushed his unruly chestnut-brown hair; his penetrating hazel-green eyes reflected back. The boy smiled as he tried on a black fedora that once belonged to his grandfather, Baruch Weiss. The hat was a little too big, so he put it aside. As he inspected the outfit his stomach felt like it was swarming with butterflies. He opened a gold-plated pocket watch that was handed down from father to son. It was half-past six, and a wintery daylight crept through a small window in the bedroom on the top floor.

Mordecai, opened his eyes and grumpily asked, "What time is it, bar mitzvah boy?"

"Going on seven. See you at the shul."

"Sure."

Ben walked down a flight of stairs and paused outside his parents' bedroom door; his father loudly snored inside. Downstairs in the kitchen, Ben's mother washed her hands and tied the strings of an apron decorated with bright yellow daffodils. She and Raisel prepared breakfast while Herschel helped his brother Arnon, feed a horse and milk a cow inside the barn. Afterward, they fed the chickens and a talkative rooster named Piros, a bright red and most annoying young bird.

"Breakfast is ready, Benjamin," his mother called from the bottom of the staircase.

"Coming."

He turned from the bedroom door, came downstairs, and placed his suit jacket and a blue velvet bag on an armchair in the hallway.

"Good morning, Mama," the boy greeted, as he entered the kitchen.

"Morning, Ben."

"How do I look?"

Hanni straightened her son's blue-striped necktie. "Handsome." She kissed his forehead. "Ready for your big day?"

"Ready as I'll ever be."

"You want some coffee?"

"Please."

Hanni placed a plate of scrambled eggs and rye toast on the table. She poured a cup of coffee for her son.

Raisel carried wood into the kitchen and stoked the cook stove. Ben watched as the flames jumped higher. She closed the iron plate on the stove top while her brother suddenly recalled the terrifying nightmare again.

"Eat your breakfast, Benjamin," his mother said, pulling him away from the dream. "What's the matter?"

"I'm nervous about my bar mitzvah."

"You'll do fine. There's no sense in worrying about it."

"Oh, you're right."

Raisel filled a bowl with oatmeal and sat beside her brother. He sprinkled a generous amount of black pepper onto his eggs; Hanni sneezed twice.

"*Gesundheit,* Mama," Raisel said.

"Thank you."

Ben scarfed down the eggs and a couple bites of toast. He pushed out the chair, got up, and drank the rest of his coffee standing.

"Why don't you finish your toast, Ben?" his mother asked.

"I don't have time."

"He doesn't have time," his mother quipped. "When did you become such an important man, Benjamin?"

He chuckled and deposited his dirty dishes into the sink. Raisel laughed and told her mother she would wash them later. The boy hurried from the kitchen and ran up the staircase, passing his father who was coming down the steps.

"Morning, Papa."

"Catching a train, Ben?"

"I'm going to the shul to practice my prayers."

"Best of luck today."

"Thanks, Papa."

* * *

Ben took a shortcut through the park, crossed a bridge, and arrived in the center of town. He quickly passed a market, a bakery, and the shop where Mr. Katz fashioned a variety of custom-made footwear and stylish leather handbags. The boy came to a building with grandiose architecture: the great synagogue of Beregszász. Ben reverently touched a silver-plated mezuzah on the doorpost, entered and covered his head with a white yarmulke before resting on a pew inside the main sanctuary. With his prayer book in hand, Ben gazed at the lofty, blue-domed ceiling, enjoying the quietude of the chapel. He closed his eyes and meditated a few moments. He sensed a mysterious presence above him. When Ben reopened his eyes, he suddenly saw a flutter of brilliant blue light on the domed ceiling. *What was that?* He picked up his skullcap which had fallen on the floor and returned it to his head. He looked up at the blue ceiling once more; nothing remained of what he had seen. Gold streaks of sunlight flashed through a stained-glass window high atop the eastern wall. The cantor and the rabbi walked into the sanctuary, and they saw Ben deeply lost in thought.

"Ah, very good ... the bar mitzvah boy has arrived early," Rabbi Schwartz announced.

"What's the matter, Benjamin? You look like you've just seen a ghost," a red-bearded Cantor Lexarman stated.

"Good Shabbos," the boy greeted the two clergymen. And they firmly shook hands.

"We don't have much time, Ben," the cantor said. "Let's do a quick run through your Haftorah."

Ben and the cantor walked to the podium, where they both unzipped velvet bags and removed their black-and-white prayer shawls. Ben recited a blessing and kissed two ends of the long tallis. He wrapped the fringed garment around his back, neck, and shoulders while the red-bearded cantor performed the same ritual with his own prayer shawl. They sat and rehearsed some of the boy's prayers.

A buzz of excitement filled the sanctuary as Ben's mother and father entered the old building and seated themselves in a front pew. Their three daughters and four sons sat in the row behind them. Friends, relatives, and neighbors were all seated amongst the large congregation. The cantor walked to the podium and sang the beginning of the Sabbath morning service, the *Shacharit.* Afterward, Ben stood on the bimah and read a portion of the Torah; his high-pitched voice rang through the sanctuary and spiraled up to the blue-domed ceiling, where unseen angels caught his devotions and delivered them up to God. Benjamin Weiss was no longer a boy that day, but a man. He ended his Haftorah, closed the book, and sat on a red velvet chair on the podium. The talkative congregation chattered from their hard wooden seats. A baby cried as an elderly gentleman appeared at the foot of the podium, requesting silence by rapping on his hard-covered book. The mother carried the crying infant out of the sanctuary while the rabbi solemnly approached the lectern and adjusted his long hanging tallis. He turned to Ben and smiled at him reassuringly. The rabbi cleared his throat before delivering a lengthy sermon.

While Cantor Lexarman chanted the *Musaf* (the concluding part of the Sabbath morning service), Hanni admired the bouquets of red roses on both sides of the podium; sunlight played upon their silky petals while Ben occasionally watched his mother's face glow with pride. His bearded and dreamy-eyed father stared up at the blue-domed ceiling, fondly recalling his own bar mitzvah in the very same sanctuary. Mendel turned a page and softly sang along to the final hymn of the service, the Adon Olam:

> The Lord of all did reign supreme
>
> before this world was made and formed.
>
> When all was finished by His will,
>
> then was His name as King proclaimed.
>
> And should these forms no longer exist,
>
> He still shall rule in majesty.
>
> He was, He is, He will remain.
>
> His glory never shall decrease.
>
> And one is He,
>
> and none there is
>
> to be compared or joined to Him.
>
> He never began, and never will end.
>
> To Him belongs dominion's power.

He is my God, my living God.

To Him I flee when tried in grief.

My banner high, my refuge strong.

He hears and answers when I call.

My spirit I commit to Him.

My body, too, and all I prize,

both when I sleep and when I awake.

He is with me; I shall have no fear.

The prayer service ended, and Rabbi Schwartz reached for a silver wine goblet and a bottle from a shelf inside the lectern. He poured a small measure of sweet red wine, raised the cup, and recited the benediction: "Blessed are You, O Lord, King of the Universe, who has created the fruit of the vine."

The congregants responded, "Amen."

The rabbi had a sip of wine, and he returned the bottle and the half-filled cup to the lectern. Ben exhaled a deep sigh of relief as the two clergymen approached him and shook his hand, extolling him with their heartfelt praises. The three men stepped off the podium, and the congregants and Ben's family members eagerly congratulated him.

Later that evening in the synagogue, Ben's parents hosted a party celebrating their son's bar mitzvah.

Mendel and his good friend Jacob Katz, stood near a table with bottles of wine, whiskey, vodka, and schnapps. Cookies, cakes, and fruit, as well as a stainless-steel coffee urn steamed on another table. Their wives sat nearby, chatting, and drinking coffee. Mendel picked up a bottle of whiskey and poured some into two shot glasses. He and his friend lifted their drinks high and toasted.

"L'chaim, Jacob."

"And a *mazel tov* to your son," the shoemaker added.

"Thank you."

They drank and the fiery beverage warmed their insides. Mendel poured more whiskey.

Mr. Katz shook his head and deeply sighed.

"You know something, Mendel?"

"What's that, Jacob?"

"I'm concerned about this hoodlum from Germany."

"Who are you referring to?" Mendel inquired.

"Klaus von Hellmenz. That loud-mouth bum in charge of the Nazi party. Last night, I heard him on my short-wave radio. He was giving a speech in Berlin. To a large crowd of his supporters."

"Nu . . . what did you hear, Katz?"

"He's a very charismatic speaker, apparently. My German isn't as good as yours, Mendel. But from what I understood, the man doesn't like German Jews all that much. Or the Jews living in the rest of Europe for that matter. He kept on mentioning the final solution. *Die Endlösung der Judenfrage.*"

"I've heard about it," Mendel said. "He wants to get rid of all the Jews from Europe."

"And where does he think the Jewish people should live? On the moon?"

Mendel laughed while his friend tilted the whiskey bottle and refilled their shot glasses again.

"I don't know about you, Katz, but I'm not buying any of Mr. Hellmenz's crazy propaganda. That worm should crawl back into the hole he came from."

"I completely agree with you, Mendel. But if the Communists aren't elected, that worm may become the new chancellor of Germany soon."

"Another fascist dictator Europe doesn't need," Mendel stated.

"My sentiments exactly."

"*L'chaim,*" the two men toasted once more.

After the two friends drank, they held each other's arm and slowly danced in a circle until they became dizzy and exhausted. The band ended their last song of the evening, and the three musicians—a male violinist, a man who played the drums, and a female accordion player who sang—left the stage and finally sat down to eat their dinner of brisket, potato pancakes, and vegetables.

Mendel and Jacob poured themselves some coffee and sat at the table with their wives.

"Let's go, Mendel. Put on your coat; we're leaving," his wife said.

Mr. Katz frowned.

"We're going too," Ruth Katz announced.

Mendel protested, but to no avail.

"The night is still young, Hanni."

"The party is finished, Mendel. You both drank enough whiskey for two nights."

Hanni handed Mendel his top hat and helped him put on his overcoat.

"I'm terribly sorry, Jacob," Mendel said.

"Don't worry, Mendel... we'll have plenty more happy occasions to celebrate. Weddings for your two daughters and a bar mitzvah for Herschel are yet to come. Which reminds me... I need to make Raisel and Zipporah high heels soon. They're beautiful women now. Men are beginning to take an interest in them."

"Never mind their interest, Mr. Katz. Let's go, Mendel," Hanni said as she tugged on her husband's arm.

"You too, Jacob," the shoemaker's wife nagged.

Mendel took out his wallet and paid the caterer and the band before they left.

"Mama, Papa," Ben greeted as the two couples congregated in the foyer of the synagogue.

Mr. Katz interrupted him. "Ah, the bar mitzvah boy himself. And how does it feel to be a man, Benjamin?"

"It feels great, Mr. Katz. Thank you for asking."

"I'm happy for you, son."

"Are you riding home with us, Benjamin?" his mother asked.

"No, I'll be home later—my friends and I are going for a walk through town."

"Don't stay out too late, Ben," his father said as he secured his black top hat and opened the large front door for his wife and Mr. and Mrs. Katz. The two couples cautiously descended the synagogue steps to the sidewalk, where they bid each other a good night.

Mr. Katz and his wife proceeded to their home close by, while Mendel and Hanni approached a horse and wagon parked alongside the curb. They observed a star-filled sky while Munka, the horse, clapped her hoof against the pavement and snorted a misty-white breath. Mendel helped his wife onto the wagon, then climbed up himself. He straightened his hat, shook the reins, and then made a clicking sound with his tongue. The strong, chocolate-colored mare trotted away from the shul, onto a main street that was paved with dull red cobblestones. The horse-drawn wagon traveled a kilometer or more, stopping on a bridge over the Verke River, the magical spot Mendel proposed to his wife twenty-four years before. She entwined her arm around his and rested her head against his shoulder. They reminisced awhile as some bats flew overhead. Mendel gave the reins a shake, and the horse and wagon crossed over the bridge, into a park illuminated by faint orange gaslights. Brittle poplar leaves crackled beneath the horse's hooves; a sudden swirl of wind swept some yellow leaves into the air, and a solitary leaf landed and stuck onto Mendel's coat sleeve, unnoticed.

"You know, Hanni . . . we're not as young as we used to be."

"You're telling me?" she said, shivering. "Come on, Mendel, I'm cold."

He rattled the reins again, and Munka broke into a slightly faster gait. They left the gaslit park behind . . . along with their fond memories.

The horse loped along a narrow lane, stopping by Mendel and Hanni's modest three-story stucco house. He drove through the open wrought-iron gate and halted near the barn; a half moon rose above its roof. He got off the wagon then helped his wife down. She brushed away the poplar leaf which had clung to her husband's coat sleeve. The bright moon glow formed silvery-yellow halos around their heads. They embraced and kissed for a moment.

"I'll be in soon, Hanni. I have to take care of the animals."

"Don't be long, Mendel."

Hanni entered the house, hung up her coat and scarf, and then pulled off her brown leather gloves. She noticed an amber light shine from the library nearby. A fire burned in a hearth inside. Her oldest son, Ignatz, was reading a book in front of the fireplace. Two kerosene lamps provided him additional light.

"Hello, sweetheart," his mother greeted the tall dark-haired man.

"Good evening, Mama. Papa in the barn?"

She nodded and went over to warm her strong but aging hands by the fireplace.

"You left the party early. What's the matter, Ignatz?"

"I wasn't feeling well."

"I'm going to make some hot tea with honey and lemon," his mother said, combing her fingers through her son's hair. "You want a cup?"

"I would like that. Thank you, Mama." Her son smiled and turned a page in the book he was reading.

The light of the fire cast his tall shadow on the wall beside him.

Outside, Mendel stood and contemplated the moon before unbridling Munka and leading her into the barn. He brushed her down before pouring fresh water into two separate troughs. The horse and milk cow drank while the rooster keenly observed them from his roost. Mendel said good night to the animals and carried a kerosene lantern out and closed the sliding wood doors of the barn. Before entering the house, he washed his hands under the water spigot in the yard.

Hanni placed two steaming cups of tea on the kitchen table. Mendel sat, added a spoonful of honey to his cup, and then stirred in a slow, deliberate manner.

"It's nice and warm in here," he said.

"Ignatz built a fire in the library."

"He's been awfully quiet lately."

"He's not feeling well," Hanni stated.

"Oh?"

"I gave him aspirin and tea."

"Good. Benjamin did a magnificent job on his Torah reading this morning."

"I'm proud of him," Hanni said. "I think the rabbi's sermon was too long."

"They usually are."

Seated opposite her husband, Hanni sipped the hot tea and thought about their oldest daughter, Pearl. She put down her cup and rubbed her arthritic hands.

"Pearl wants to go to America," Hanni announced.

Mendel pretended not to hear what she just said, while he gazed out the kitchen window and thought of what he had to do for work the next day. He drummed a teaspoon against his cup.

"Mendel?"

"*Igen*, Hanni?"

"Stop that. It's annoying me. Did you hear what I said?"

"Everybody wants to go to America someday, Hanni."

"I didn't say everybody."

"Who wants to go to America?"

"Pearl—."

"Sorry, I was daydreaming."

"You drank too much whiskey, Mendel."

"Oh, leave me alone already. I was celebrating. How many times will Benjamin have a bar mitzvah?"

Mendel took his cigarettes from his shirt pocket and lit one. He reached for the Hungarian newspaper, the Magyar Nemzet. His dignified jaw locked as he blankly stared at the front page. A photograph displayed a man dressed in a full military uniform; his arm was stiffly raised with a red, black, and white armband tied around it. The man's face looked as if it had been bitten by a rabid dog. A headline was printed above the photograph:

Klaus von Hellmenz elected Chancellor of Germany

"Have you seen this yet, Hanni?"

"What?"

"That Nazi politician was appointed the new chancellor of Germany today."

He showed her the unwelcome news on the front page.

"He has a scary looking face," she remarked.

"He doesn't look like a kindhearted man—that's for sure."

Mendel yawned, dejectedly folded the newspaper, and then put out the cigarette.

"What were you saying about Pearl?" he asked. "She can't go flouncing off on vacation. Especially such a long distance from home."

"She's not going on vacation, Mendel. She wants to live in America."

"Why?"

"Pearl doesn't like it in Beregszász anymore," Hanni replied.

"I don't either. Do you see me running off to America? And where does Pearl plan to live once she gets there?

"In Newburgh, New York. Where your brother lives. She can stay at his house until she finds a small apartment. Your brother agreed to sponsor her. He mentioned it in the last telegram he sent us—don't you remember?"

"*Igen*. I recall now," Mendel replied. "Pearl will need a green card. And she'll have to work somewhere."

"She knows."

Hanni bit into a chocolate-filled kokosh she had saved from the party. Mendel lit himself another cigarette and had a sip of tea. He sighed.

"I wish you would stop smoking already. America is the land of opportunity. Your brother became successful there. And I heard that most of the houses have indoor plumbing now."

"I suppose all the streets in America are paved with gold?"

"Only the sidewalks. Don't be ridiculous, Mendel. Besides—if Germany starts another war—we may all have to leave Beregszász eventually."

"Those are only crazy rumors, Hanni. Germany is much too busy rebuilding their country from the last war. Does Zipporah want to go to America also?"

Tears welled up in the short but strong woman's brown eyes. "I told her she couldn't leave home until she finished school."

"Oh, Hanni . . . don't cry. How fast our little girls have grown up."

"Our boys too," she added, wiping her tears. "Why don't you go to bed, Mendel. You're probably exhausted. Where are you working tomorrow?"

"Jacob wants me to pick up some boxes from the leather factory, and I'll have to drive to Uzhhorod afterwards."

"For what reason?"

"A customer owes me some money. I'll stop by Hugo's farm and bring back a few sacks of vegetables."

"Buy some tomatoes and cabbage," his wife requested. "And take the lantern with you—you'll be coming home in the dark—I'll pack you a supper."

"When will Pearl go to America, Hanni?"

"When she has enough money saved for a ticket on the steamship."

"How much does a ticket cost?"

"A one-way second-class ticket from Trieste to New York would be a hundred and sixty American dollars."

"Why a one-way ticket?" Mendel asked while he wrinkled his forehead, feeling a deep sadness in his heart.

"She's not coming back to Beregszász, sweetheart."

"Oh?"

"No."

Tears rolled down Mendel's cheeks; he removed a handkerchief from the pocket of his dress shirt, then dabbed the moisture.

"Pearl will be okay, Mendel. Don't worry. She's a grown-up woman. She can look after herself. And she speaks good English."

"I know. Where's Trieste, Hanni?"

"On the northeast coast of Italy. She will have to take a train from Budapest to get there."

Mendel pushed out his chair and tiredly stood; his balance was a little shaky.

"Pearl doesn't have to worry about the money, Hanni. I will buy her a first-class ticket. Where is Benjamin?" he asked.

"Still out with his friends. I'll stay up until he comes home."

"I'm going to bed then." Mendel gently kissed the top of his wife's head. "Good night, Hanni."

"Sleep tight, Mendel. I love you."

"I love you too."

*Note to the reader: Klaus von Hellmenz, is a fictitious name. He represents the real person {the Fuhrer} who was in charge of the Nazi Party, before and during the Second World War. For personal reasons, I chose not to use his actual name in the book.

3

On a soccer field in Beregszász, Ben stood a few meters from the ball and faced the opposing team's goalkeeper. He anxiously waited for a stripe-shirted referee to give him the signal for a penalty kick, which could determine the outcome of the amateur league soccer tournament. Ben placed his full attention on the ball while the goalie mockingly waved his arms from side to side and up and down, attempting to arouse a nervousness in the man from Beregszász. There were only five more seconds left on the game clock before the match might go into overtime. The score was tied two-all between the reigning league champions, a flashy-colored and hot-shot team from Budapest, and a tough, dark-horse squad, the host from Beregszász. Ben played center midfielder for the underdogs. His team wore plain white T-shirts; black, white, or brown socks; and drab shorts of mismatched colors. Budapest's team flaunted navy-blue jerseys with muddied white numerals, gray shorts, white socks, and proper black athletic shoes.

It was nothing short of a miracle the Beregszász team had qualified for the quarterfinals, semi-finals, and now the finals.

Ben shut out everything around him while he took deep breaths, dug his heels into the turf, leaned forward, and then rested a hand on his knee; his adrenaline pumped hard. The ref blew the whistle and Ben sprinted for the ball. His timing was perfect; he kicked it straight for the goal at bullet speed. The overly confident goaltender thought it would be easily caught or knocked away, but at the very last moment, the ball mysteriously swerved right, then jumped past the goalie's hands and into the upper-left corner of the net. Ben raised his arms high as the goalie dropped flat on his face and angrily pounded his fists on the wet ground. The referee signaled the kick was good.

"Goal!" The Beregszász fans and teammates on the bench yelled and jumped up and down.

The game ended with looks of horror on the faces of the other team's coach, players, and fans. Thunder sounded, and a light rain dropped onto the field. Ben's coach and teammates ecstatically mobbed him, lifting him onto their shoulders and parading him across the dampened turf. After the league's president awarded the Beregszás team the championship trophy, the defeated Budapest squad warmly congratulated them. The head referee patted Ben's shoulder and gave him the game ball as a memento. Mendel and Mr. Katz came down from the bleachers and approached the bench on the sideline.

"Great kick, son!" Ben's father exclaimed.

"A wonderful goal," Mr. Katz stated. "And perfectly placed, if I may add."

Ben looked up while he untied his soccer shoes.

"Thanks . . . I prayed it wouldn't go over."

"God must have been listening to you," Mr. Katz said.

"Amazing kick, Ben," his team's goalkeeper said, giving him a firm handshake.

"Thanks, Chubac."

"Think about what I told you before," the goalkeeper said, looking deeply into Ben's hazel-green eyes. He released his grip.

"I will, Chubac. See you at practice next week."

"Yeah . . ."

"Would you like a ride home with me?" Ben's father asked.

"Sure, give me a couple minutes, Papa."

"I'll see you two later," Mr. Katz said. "And give my regards to Hanni."

"And ours to Ruth," Mendel said. "Coffee tomorrow morning, Jacob?"

"*Igen*. I'll see you bright and early."

Mendel's old brown mare sluggishly trotted away from the field, pulling the wagon behind. Ben opened an umbrella and shielded him and his father from a heavy rain. A clamorous railroad bell rang when they neared a crossing; the horse stopped well before the wooden barrier as a slow-moving freight train sounded its horn. The horse neighed and shook her head up and down while an iron-black locomotive chugged past with its graffiti-smeared box cars.

"Munka, it's okay," Mendel comfortingly told the horse. "I have to admit, son, it looked like the game was going into overtime."

"Why? You thought the goalie had a save?"

"You fooled me for a moment," Mendel answered. "Any higher, the ball would've hit the crossbar. I've watched you make that kick before. And not always successfully."

"It's too bad Mama didn't see the game," Ben mentioned.

"Maybe next time."

"Hear any more news about the war, Papa?"

"The Germans invaded France and Belgium this morning."

"Oh?"

"I heard it on the BBC, from Katz's short-wave radio. I hope we're not in danger, Ben."

The young man thought as he watched the dirty freight cars roll past. *We should have left Hungary two years ago. There aren't any passenger ships leaving Europe now. Why were we so naive?*

Mendel looked at his son. "What was your teammate, Chubac, talking to you about earlier?"

"He told me the secret police are arresting Jews all over Germany. There's been a lot of violence lately."

"Oh?"

"*Igen.* They're putting German Jews onto trains and taking them to forced labor camps. Some as far as Poland. The Nazis have closed and smashed the windows of Jewish businesses. Broken glass everywhere. In Frankfurt, Munich, and Berlin. It may not be safe for us in Hungary anymore, Papa."

"Fucking bastards," Mendel said before lighting a cigarette. Munka sneezed from the smoke. "Why can't they leave the Jewish people alone?"

"I don't know, Papa. They always need someone to blame their troubles on."

"This is true."

A string of boxcars passed the horse's nose while Mendel tightly clenched the reins with one hand and nervously smoked with the other.

"How does your teammate Chubac know all this information?"

"He gets the news firsthand. His uncle works at the German consulate in Budapest."

"Maybe it's time for the rest of our family to leave for America, no?" Mendel said.

"How, Papa? It's too dangerous crossing the Atlantic now. German U-boats are sinking anything that floats. Even if we found a passenger ship to sail on . . . we'd be risking our lives."

"Perhaps we could take a boat from Greece?" Mendel asked. "And go to Israel. Katz told me that many Jews from Hungary have gone that route. We could start a new life in the promised land."

"We'd have to travel through Italy to reach Greece," Ben replied. "That might've been possible a few months ago, but now that Italy has become an ally of Germany, I'm not so sure it's a good idea."

"I forgot about that. Eh. Why should we even worry about it, son? The Germans don't dare invade Hungary. Our army is too strong—besides, the war can't go on much longer. The American and allied forces will rip them to shreds like the last war."

"I hope you're right," Ben said as the final box car and caboose pushed a wet air into their faces.

The railroad bell stopped clanging, and the wooden crossing bar went up. A Hungarian army truck drove past from the opposite direction. Mendel cast his burning cigarette away and carefully navigated the horse and wagon across the bumpy tracks, then into the center of town. They slowly passed the great synagogue, the butcher shop, the tailor's window, the fish market, Mr. Katz's shoe store, and then Mendel stopped at the large brick post office on William Street. When the bearded man with the top hat climbed down from the wagon, he splashed his work boots into a dark puddle.

"I have to pick up a package, Ben," Mendel said as his old work horse sadly looked up at him.

"Oh."

"You can give Munka an apple. I'll be back in a few minutes."

Mendel straightened his coat collar and adjusted his top hat before going inside the large brick building. He opened the door and immediately felt a strange premonition. He stood in a line behind an old woman who had a battered suitcase by her side. She looked back at him. Mendel smiled and tipped his top hat. The haggardly old woman frowned while she made the sign of the cross. She turned and faced the clerk's window again. Mendel shrugged.

Outside the post office, Ben grabbed two golden delicious apples from a covered box in the back; he offered the horse one, and she leisurely chomped it down. Ben contemplated Munka's melancholic eyes; she seemed to question him. She looks as if she wants to tell me something important; perhaps only a horse would have a sense of knowing. I wonder what she's thinking about. Probably doesn't have many years left. She's old now. I was just a little boy when I first saw her. She was young and strong then. Papa was too. Ben fondly stroked Munka's chocolate-brown coat speckled gray now. He smelled her earthy equine odor in the fresh air as he climbed back on the wagon. Ben polished his apple, took a bite, and relished the sweet juice. The clouds partially dispersed, and the afternoon rays reflected in the rain puddles. A faint band of colors appeared in the sky.

"Tasty apples, hah, Munka?" Ben asked.

The horse snorted and tapped her front hoof upon the cobblestone.

Back inside the post office, the old woman who stood in front of Mendel took her mail and grabbed the handle on her suitcase. When she passed, she gave him an ill-humored glance and spit on the floor. He pursed his lips and raised his eyebrows. *Why would she do such a thing?* he pondered. He heard the blond-haired mail clerk shout:

"Next in line!"

Mendel approached the window.

"Identification," the mail clerk rudely requested.

Mr. Weiss handed over his identity card. "Everyone knows me in Beregszász," he calmly stated.

The clerk didn't answer at first, scrutinizing the identification card. He coldly looked up at Mendel.

"I don't know you," the clerk curtly answered.

"Mr. Gotlieb usually works at this window—is he on vacation?"

"His job was terminated yesterday. Take your card. Jews will no longer be employed at the post office, or any other municipal jobs in Hungary for that matter. No more questions."

Mendel stood there bewildered. Once again, he felt a ghostly air rest above his shoulders. Sunlight shone through a large window, forming a strange white circle on the dark marble floor; Mendel stared at it a few moments. The postal clerk returned and placed on the counter a medium-size box and a white envelope with foreign postage stamps on it.

"Sign your name," the clerk said.

Mendel scribbled his signature on a slip, collected the mail, and then slowly exited the building. He placed the box under a tarp in the wagon, then gave his son the envelope. They rode home in silence.

* * *

Ben excitedly entered the kitchen with the soccer ball tucked under his arm; he tossed the envelope onto the table, smelling a pungent aroma of food. His mother greeted him from the stove.

"Hello, Benjamin."

"Mama—we won the finals! I scored the winning goal. We beat Budapest!"

His mother kept stirring something in a large, cast-iron pot. She covered it, and said with no more ado, "That's wonderful, Benjamin."

Disappointed by his mother's lackluster response, Ben awkwardly stood there, noticing her wrinkled forehead and dispirited stance. Her face appeared to have aged since he saw her in the morning.

"What's the matter, Mama?"

"Nothing. Go wash up and get ready for supper."

"What are we having?"

"Stuffed cabbage. Where's your father?" she asked, peeling a cucumber.

"In the barn."

Ben's sister, Raisel, entered the kitchen with a laundry basket full of clothes she had taken off the line in the backyard.

"Hi, Ben."

"Hi, Raisel."

"I watched the first half of your game. Did your team win?"

"Yes ... three to two. I scored the winning goal on a penalty kick."

"Wow—that's terrific!"

"I'll tell you all about it after supper."

* * *

Mendel used the outhouse, then washed his hands at the water pump outside. He wiped his muddy work boots on a mat before taking them off by the front door. He entered the house, hung up his coat, scarf, and hat, and then greeted his wife in the kitchen.

"I get any calls, Hanni?"

"No."

Mendel picked up the stamped envelope on the table and saw who it was from.

"Mr. Katz sends his regards," he told his wife.

"That's nice."

"Ben's team won the championship. He scored the winning goal," Mendel said while sitting.

"He told me when he came in," she said, cutting up a kohlrabi. She bit into the hard vegetable, then gave her husband a piece. "What's that?" she asked, noticing the purple-and-white postage stamps on the envelope.

"Mail from America."

"From your brother?"

"No, Zipporah sent it. Should I open it?"

"Go ahead. I'm through cooking."

Hanni gave her husband a butter knife, and he unsealed the envelope. He removed the folded letter and handed it to his wife. Mendel drank some cold coffee from the morning.

"*Nu.* What are you waiting for?" he asked.

"All right. Let me sit down first."

Hanni untied her apron and draped it over a chair. She sat and unfolded the one-page letter that was written in Hungarian. She discovered a crisp hundred-dollar bill inside a folded piece of newspaper. She happily showed the money to her husband, who smiled while his wife cleaned and adjusted her reading glasses.

Dear Mama and Papa,

Greetings from America. I hope you're all well. Because of the war my letter was probably delayed a long time. I'm fine, but it's bitter cold in Newburgh right now. We had two snowstorms in one week. Spring is around the corner, though. And the apple trees will blossom soon. I miss everyone. Wish you could leave Hungary and come to Newburgh, but that may not be possible until the war is over. I pray you'll be safe in Beregszász. Next month my citizenship papers should arrive. I'm so excited! My job in the bakery is difficult. The hours are long, and the pay is minimum wage. Papa always said that money doesn't grow on trees. He was right. I visit Pearl whenever I get the chance. She sends her love. I have a boyfriend now. He owns a grocery store in Newburgh. A nice Jewish man named Benny. On my day off he took me on my first train trip to Manhattan. Broadway was amazing! Shows and movie theaters everywhere. All kinds of restaurants and clothing stores. I never dreamed New York City would be so much fun. The buildings are so tall there, I felt like a tiny ant. What crowds of people. Will send you photographs in my next letter. Hugs and kisses to all.

Love,

Zipporah

Hanni folded the letter and placed it back inside the envelope. She glanced at her husband's melancholic disposition. He turned away and reached for a cigarette while tears rolled down his cheeks.

"What's the matter, Mendel—why you crying?"

"I'm glad Zipporah is happy in America. I only wish we could be there also."

"I know. Put away the money. We'll eat soon. I'll be right back."

Hanni went out the kitchen door to the backyard. Piros, the friendly old rooster, hobbled past her short, quivering legs; the bird quietly muttered to himself, while a songbird rustled in an apple tree nearby. Hanni watched as a big apricot-colored sun dropped behind the barn. She buried her face in her hands and cried.

4

Six Years Later

May 25, 1944

The drivers of a Hungarian army truck and a German military vehicle, a *Kübelwagen,* abruptly braked in front of a busy food market on a main street in Beregszász. Two Hungarian soldiers climbed off the truck while three Nazi soldiers got out of the other vehicle; they noticed a couple of ultra-orthodox Jewish men who were browsing through an outdoor fruit-and-vegetable stall. Yellow Stars of David were sewn onto the men's garments. The Hungarian soldiers entered the market to buy whiskey and cigarettes while the three stubble-faced Gestapo approached the two bearded Jews dressed in long black coats and strange fur hats known as shtreimels.

A blond and blue-eyed Nazi named Sergeant Heimlich, sharply addressed the Jews in a heavy Nurembergian accent, "Hey! What are you doing here, *Juden?*"

"Buying food for our families," the taller Jew answered. "*Iz das* a crime?"

"*Muterfucker!*" the sergeant shouted, "*Verboten!* You are violating the curfew. You should be home."

A Captain Manheim added insult to injury. "Or in the ghetto where you belong. *Schmutzig Juden.*"

The taller man remained calm in the face of being called a dirty Jew. He replied in a broken German and Yiddish, "I'm sorry, but we didn't know there was a curfew. Please—let us buy some food—then we will go home to our families. I have eight *kinder* and my wife to feed. My friend, Shmeil has six *kinder* plus his *muter* and *fater.* Everyone is starving."

"*Nein!*" the sergeant shrieked as he knocked off the man's funny looking round hat and punched him in the nose so hard, it bled. The Jew staggered backward but remained upright. He held a white cloth to his bleeding nose. The shorter Jew picked up and brushed off his friend's black fur hat before giving it to him.

Customers nearby watched in shock as children and infants cried. The Gestapo laughed while the owner of the market came out and forced a smile. He apologized to customers, comforting the children by handing them lollipops and chewing gum.

"Now look what you've done, *Juden.* You've upset the *kinder,*" Captain Manheim gently spoke as he patted a little boy's head. His mother quickly grabbed her son's hand and walked away.

"*Schmutzig Juden.* You're both under arrest," the sergeant announced.

"But we didn't know there was a curfew," the shorter Chasid stated.

"Shut up your mouth, Jew!" a Nazi corporal named Wagner yelled.

The three Gestapo pulled the two Jews to the middle of the sidewalk, where they took out barber scissors and hacked off their lengthy beards and side-locks. Before they continued with their business, inquisitive pedestrians and shop customers pitied or laughed at the humiliated Jews. The two Hungarian soldiers arrived at the scene and started kicking the beardless men onto the back of the flatbed army truck, already laden with families from Beregszász.

"Take us to the next location," Captain Manheim ordered the driver of the army truck.

"*Jawohl, Capitan.*"

* * *

The Hungarian army truck and German *Kübelwagen* jerked up and down the cobblestone street while the thirty-plus passengers on the flatbed truck knocked against one another and struggled to keep from falling off. The jeep-like vehicle and truck bounced over the Verke Bridge, through Gorky Park, and then onto a more rural Bereg Street. The Hungarian soldier waved his hand out the truck window and both vehicles parked in front of a modest three-story stucco house. The driver got out with his clipboard and approached the Gestapo captain.

"I know the owner of this house," the soldier told the captain. "He used to deliver bags of produce to my brother's restaurant. My boy played on the soccer team with his son. They won the league championship a few years ago. Against Budapest," the Hungarian soldier proudly stated.

"Oh, really?" the captain congenially asked while casually exhaling some nasty smelling cigarette smoke into the Hungarian man's face.

"Do you want us to bring them out?" the soldier questioned Captain Manheim.

"*Nein*—we will take care of it," he snapped. "What's the owner's name?"

"Mendel Weiss, *Capitan.*"

"Mendel Veiss?" he said, his accent making the *w* sound like a *v.*

"*Igen*," the soldier affirmed in Hungarian.

"Drop this load off at the factory," the captain ordered. "And pick up more Jews afterwards. Come back in one hour. And don't be late."

"*Jawohl*," the Hungarian soldier said as he checked his wristwatch. The man climbed back into the smoke-filled truck cab and snatched a whiskey bottle from the other soldier, having himself a drink before yanking the gear shift and rocking the truck down the stone-paved lane. The two Hungarian soldiers laughed along the way.

The Gestapo trio climbed from the military vehicle and viewed Mendel Weiss' well-kept residence behind a tall, wrought-iron gate. Sergeant Heimlich shot the lock off with his Lugar pistol. A feisty old rooster screamed when it heard the loud pop; the horse neighed, and Mendel's dairy cow almost kicked over a bucket of milk Ben had filled only a minute before the soldiers arrived. His brother, Mordecai, hid himself beneath a haystack while Ben ran out of the barn and bolted toward the house. Sergeant Heimlich smiled, holstered his pistol, and then kicked open the Weiss' iron gate. The high-booted Gestapo casually swaggered onto the sweet-smelling property. Captain Manheim unzipped his pants, pulled out his prick, and then urinated under a blossoming apple tree. He admired the pinkish-white blossoms while Sergeant Heimlich relieved himself onto Hanni's favorite rose bush. A near-sighted Corporal Wagner focused through his coke-bottle eyeglasses, curious about the barn ahead of him. He approached it.

Ben stood breathless after closing the kitchen door. His heart pounded.

"What was that noise, Benjamin?" his mother asked. "And why haven't you milked the cow yet? —you know I have to make butter today."

"I did the milking already. Soldiers are here," he quietly announced.

"Oh my God. Where is Mordecai?"

"Hiding in the barn."

Mendel threw down his newspaper. "What happened, son?"

"Lower your voice, Mendel," his wife pleaded.

"Someone fired a gun," Ben whispered.

"Hungarian soldiers?" his father asked.

"I think Nazis," Ben replied as he wiped some perspiration from his forehead. "I heard them speaking German."

"God help us," his father whispered.

Raisel and her younger brother, thirteen-year-old Herschel, came downstairs in their pajamas.

"What's all the commotion about, Mama?" she asked while Herschel peeked through the kitchen window.

"Soldiers are outside."

"Quiet, everyone," Mendel ordered. "Get away from there, Herschel. Go upstairs with your sister and hide in the closet. And don't make a sound. Ben—go to the basement."

"I'll stay here with you and Mama."

"We have to remain calm," Mendel said. "Make coffee, Hanni. Our guests may be visiting us soon."

"*Igen.*"

Raisel and Herschel ran up the staircase. Hanni poured hot water from the stove into her largest coffee percolator while Ben took a broom and swept the floor in the hallway. Mendel lit a cigarette. And nervously opened the newspaper.

* * *

In the barn, the poor-sighted corporal kicked away the rooster, and he accidentally stepped into a full bucket of milk, drenching his boot, sock, and pants. He angrily swore at the cow in German, "*Verdammte kuh!*"

Mordecai's underarms sweat profusely as he drew a shallow breath under the scratchy haystack.

The captain entered the barn and noticed the corporal's wet pants. "You pissed your pants, Wagner?"

"That fucking milk pail was in my way!" he exclaimed as his face changed color.

"That was clumsy of you."

"I didn't see it."

"Perhaps you should get yourself some stronger lenses. Hey, Corporal?" the captain asked.

"I found a pump for water on the other side of the barn," the sergeant announced as he entered the barn. "What happened to you, Wagner?" he asked, noticing the corporal's dampened boots and trousers.

"I had an accident."

The captain and the sergeant had a good laugh while the corporal kicked some hay and continued to swear. Mordecai held his breath.

"Let's drink water. I'm very thirsty," the captain stated. "And the corporal can change his diaper."

While the three Gestapo gathered at the water pump in the yard, Herschel and his sister secretly watched them from an upstairs window. The men pumped out the cold water and drank. Afterward, the corporal removed his boots and stripped to his underpants. He washed his trousers and socks, then hung them on the clothesline nearby.

"I'm hungry," Captain Manheim announced. "There must be some food in the house. Shall we pay Mr. Veiss and his family a visit?"

"*Ja, das ist gut,*" the sergeant replied.

* * *

Hanni apprehensively stood by the stove, where she fried potatoes, onions, and garlic in a cast-iron pan. She sprinkled in paprika, salt and pepper, and then sneezed. Mendel sat at the kitchen table where he blankly stared at the headlines in the Magyar Nemzet newspaper. He took out a pack of cigarettes Pearl had mailed from New York. He nervously lit one.

"A German submarine was sunk in the North Sea, Ben," his father announced.

"Oh?" he replied, pensively sweeping the kitchen floor.

"Near Holland."

They heard a loud banging on the front door. The sound echoed through the house. Upstairs, Raisel and Hershel shuddered.

"I think that's our guests, Ben," Mendel said.

"Igen."

"Come in," Mendel yelled in German from the kitchen table.

Modeling his white boxer shorts with his long black boots in hand, the corporal followed after the other two Nazis. They entered the home and observed a framed portrait of Mendel and Hanni's smiling family on the wall in the foyer: Mendel, his wife, five sons and three daughters. The sergeant saw the black and white photograph, ripped it off the wall, and then smashed the glass-covered picture under his boot. While the corporal investigated the library, the captain and the sergeant stomped down the hall and stoically gathered at the threshold of the kitchen. Ben and his father locked eyes with the men. The Gestapo observed their cleanly shaved faces.

"Welcome to our humble abode, gentlemen," Mendel politely greeted in German. "The coffee is almost ready."

"*Danke schön*," the captain said.

"Can I help you with something?" Mendel inquired.

"Are you German?" the captain asked.

Mendel thought for a moment, looked at the captain and replied, "No, we are Hungarians."

"And I assume you are Jews?" the sergeant interrogated in a much less friendly tone.

An uncomfortable silence filled the kitchen a moment. Mendel thought to say they were Christians.

Standing guard with the broom, Ben replied in a resolute manner, "*Ja*. We are Jews."

"I thought so," the sergeant said, as he approached him.

Ben clenched the broom handle with his powerful hands. A much taller Sergeant Heimlich loomed over him and glared into Ben's piercing green eyes. The sergeant grabbed the broom handle and broke it in half. He placed his gun barrel against Ben's temple and easily pushed him aside. He asked him if he spoke German, "*Sprechen Sie Deutsch,* muscleman?"

"*Ja.*"

"*Gut. Auf dem boden sitzen,*" the sergeant said while pointing his gun toward a corner of the kitchen floor. Ben went over and sat. The captain and the sergeant seated themselves at the kitchen table. Both of them removed their boots, and Hanni wrinkled her nose at the soldiers' foul foot odor.

"Give us coffee and breakfast. *Schnell,*" the sergeant ordered Hanni in German. He set his pistol on the table.

She looked up puzzled. Ben translated for her, "Mama. They asked for you to make them breakfast and give them coffee."

Hanni meekly acknowledged in Hungarian, "*Igen, Capitan.*"

Mendel courteously offered the Gestapo his Marlboro cigarettes. He lit them with a silver-plated lighter.

"Ah! American cigarettes, *Danke schön,*" the captain said. "Where did you get those from?"

"New York," Mendel replied as he lit a Marlboro for himself. "My two daughters live in America. They send me sometimes from New York."

Hanni served them coffee.

The sergeant turned to Mendel and gave him a dirty look. "We are from the Secret Police," he said. "We were informed that a Mendel Weiss owns this house. Is that you?"

"Yes, my name is Weiss."

"You and your family are under arrest," the sergeant announced.

"Why? Do we look like criminals?"

"Shut up your fucking mouth, Jew-dog!" the sergeant shouted. He picked up his pistol and pointed it at Mendel. Hanni's heart almost stopped.

"Sergeant!" Captain Manheim exclaimed. "Don't be so rude. We are their guests. Put away your gun. And show them some manners. Corporal! There is coffee if you want." The captain added a spoonful of sugar to his cup and stirred.

Hanni browned some potatoes and checked the beef brisket that was warming in the oven. She took down three plates from the cupboard and forks from a drawer, placing it on the table. She cut into a challah that was left over from the previous Sabbath.

"Mendel, would you please ask the *Capitan* if I could get some fresh eggs from the barn."

"Capitan?"

"*Ja?*"

"Is it possible my wife can go to the barn for eggs?"

"Go."

The captain nodded and gestured with his hand. Hanni took a small basket and went outside through the kitchen door. She briefly noticed the strange pants and socks that were drying on the clothesline. She entered the barn and judiciously selected a dozen brown eggs. The rooster questioned her by pecking at her sandaled feet. Before leaving, Hanni glanced at the haystack and softly spoke:

"Mordecai? Are you there?"

"Mama?"

"Stay where you are, son. The Germans are in the house right now. They will arrest us. Don't come out until dark."

"Where will they take you?"

"I don't know," she replied. "There's money hidden in the attic. Under the mattress. Take it and leave Beregszász tonight. Go to Budapest. It's safer there."

"Mama— "

"I hope we will see you again. I love you, Mordecai."

* * *

The half-dressed corporal snooped around the living room and discovered a bottle of plum brandy. He drank some, took the bottle upstairs, and then ransacked the master bedroom. He searched through a dresser and found a meager amount of American dollars and Hanni's diamond wedding ring. He stashed it into his shirt pocket, gulped more liquor, and then threw the bottle into a mirror, breaking both. The loud noise frightened Herschel and Raisel, who were hiding in the closet across the room. They dared not breathe. Something fell from inside their hiding place. The corporal heard. He walked toward the closet, held onto a doorknob, and then flung open the door. Sunlight flooded in. The corporal ripped clothes off the hangers, then saw two blurred figures tightly squeezed in a corner.

"Come out!" he shouted.

The sister and brother crawled from their hiding place on hands and knees; they slowly came to their feet and raised their arms above their heads in surrender. The corporal lasciviously rolled his beady eyes over the young woman's firmly shaped body. He turned his gaze to the frightened thirteen-year-old.

"Go to the kitchen," he sternly ordered him in Hungarian.

"*Igen, Capitan.*"

Herschel did what he was told.

The corporal ripped off Raisel's pajama top, exposing her pallid breasts and coffee-brown nipples. She tried to scream, but nothing came out of her mouth. The corporal clumsily fondled the young woman's breasts while attempting to kiss her. She smelled his raunchy breath as he took out his semi-erect penis, pushed her onto the bed, and was about to climb on top, when Captain Manheim yelled from the bottom of the staircase:

"Wagner! Come down for breakfast. We're leaving soon."

The corporal returned his flaccid member to his boxer shorts, and he awkwardly put on his coke-bottle eyeglasses.

"Get dressed," he ordered the trembling young woman.

While Hanni, Raisel, and Ben washed the pots, silverware and dishes, Captain Manheim got up from the table and announced, "I'll be back in ten minutes. I have something urgent to take care of."

"Do you need my assistance, *Capitan?*" the corporal asked while he smeared some butter onto a slice of challah.

"I'm going to take a shit. You want to watch me?"

"*Nein.*"

Ben, his father, and the sergeant laughed.

"Have the older son and his sister pack some clothes for everyone, but not too much," the captain said, before he left for the outhouse.

"*Jawohl.* Go upstairs and pack," the sergeant told Ben and Raisel.

Ben and his sister went upstairs and placed some of their family's belongings onto bed sheets and tied them into bundles. Raisel threw a bra, panties, her favorite dress, and a pair of red high heels into a ragged suitcase. She closed it and secured it with twine. The brother and sister carried the packed clothes down to the living room, where they glumly looked at each other.

"I'm really afraid, Ben."

"Me too, Raisel."

"Shut up!" the sergeant yelled as the Gestapo gathered the others into the living room.

The Hungarian army truck pulled up front, and the driver beeped the horn. The other soldier tipped the whiskey bottle and drank.

"Get them out of here, Wagner," the captain ordered.

"*Ja.*"

Fully dressed, holding his pistol loosely aimed at Ben's back, the corporal led the family out the front door toward the flatbed truck. Mendel recognized one of the Hungarian soldiers and waved to him, but the soldier sadly looked away and climbed behind the wheel. Ben briefly glanced at the barn as he helped his family members onto the truck. Various passengers knew the Weiss family, somberly greeting them.

"Is that everyone, *Capitan*?" the Hungarian soldier asked from the driver's seat.

"*Ja*—now take them directly to the brick factory," the captain replied, noticing the soldiers' slapdash condition. "And this will be your last run of the day. Both of you need to sober up."

"Heil Hellmenz, Capitan."

The army truck jerked forward suddenly and stalled twice before it rocked up and down Bereg Street. Mendel and his family dismally watched their house and barn disappear while their old rooster stood beside the front gate and crowed long and loud.

Mordecai carefully listened as a few chickens clucked, his father's old horse whimpered, and then the barn became ghostly silent. The young man cautiously crawled from under the haystack and brushed off his clothes.

* * *

The Hungarian army truck slowly approached the Verke Bridge. From the calm river below, a man waved from inside a small fishing boat.

"Where are they taking us, Papa?" Raisel asked.

"God only knows, sweetheart. I'm sure it will only be temporary."

"Who will feed and give water to the animals while we're gone, Papa?"

"Hopefully one of our good Christian neighbors will look after them. For now, we have enough to worry about."

Raisel and her mother cried. Mendel securely held onto their arms. Ben sat beside his younger brother.

When the army truck approached the great synagogue of Beregszász, Ben saw that its stained-glass windows had been broken. Profanity was written on the front wall in German and Hungarian. Ugly black swastikas were painted on the doors and noble stone façade. Long benches, tables and chairs, and the ark for the Torahs had been busted up and stacked on the sidewalk for firewood. Torah scrolls, books, and prayer shawls had been thrown in disheveled piles beside the broken furniture. Young, snot-nosed children curiously picked through the mess; one of them mockingly wrapped a prayer shawl around him and ran down the street. The other kids glanced up when the army truck parked in front. A soldier got out and entered the shul. He appeared shortly after, pulling the congregation's rabbi by his beard; he still wore his tefillin and prayer shawl. His wife cried by his side as they climbed onto the truck.

The military vehicle left the center of town and crossed over some railroad tracks before driving by a weedy and unkempt athletic field. Ben fondly observed the place where he had played soccer from the time he was a boy. The driver turned onto a one-lane dirt road, beeping the horn for a group of pimple-faced children; they laughed and waved while some older, mean-faced boys cursed and threw stones at the passengers on the back of the truck. It drove on. A few minutes after, Ben recognized the Beregszász brick factory from a distance; he'd been there a couple of times with his father to deliver sacks of clay. The building had no outer walls; only pillars and beams supported its flat roof. Railroad tracks ran beside the factory. The army truck stopped in front, and the two Hungarian soldiers drunkenly climbed out, shouting at the people on the truck.

"Get off, *Juden!*"

Ben helped his family members from the truck, then he and some other young men assisted the children and elderly.

"Off!" a soldier yelled once more.

Meanwhile, another Hungarian soldier prodded an older gentleman who was wrapped in a blanket and fast asleep on the truck.

"Get up, you fucking rotten Jew-dog-bastard!"

The old man mumbled an obscenity but remained stationary. The soldier yanked him off the truck and dropped him onto the hard ground. The old man screamed as the soldier repeatedly kicked him in the ribs; someone else came along and beat him with a wooden club till he stopped breathing. Two civilian-clothed men grabbed the old man's limbs and carried him to a garbage-strewn field nearby. They dropped him into an open grave, where several other bodies lay. Shortly after, several young men filled the hole with shovelfuls of dirt. And that was that.

Meanwhile, Mendel and his family squeezed through the crowded brick factory. Ben saw a teammate from his ex-soccer team, a few neighbors, and his boss from the glass shop. Everyone was corralled inside like sheep. Men, women, and older children read from prayer books, as if they were in the synagogue—

chanting hymns, beating their chests, and crying out loud. Ben caught a glimpse of Cantor Lexarman, the man who had officiated at his bar mitzvah several years ago. He stretched his neck, but the cantor's troubled eyes and grayish red beard soon vanished within the crowd.

"It stinks in here," Hanni said, wrinkling her brow as she clamped her nose shut.

"I see Mr. Katz and his wife, Papa," Ben announced. "There's a space next to them."

"Let's go, everyone," Mendel said.

Ben held onto his father's arm as they neared the shoemaker and his wife. They were seated on the dirt floor, and a blanket was draped over Mrs. Katz. She coughed and shivered. Mendel and his family awkwardly approached. Mr. Katz's wife momentarily opened her eyes; she barely managed a faint hello and a brief smile.

"Hello, Jacob," Mendel greeted.

"Mendel, Hanni, Ben, Raisel, Herschel. I'm so happy to see you all," Mr. Katz said. "You just arrived?"

"Not long ago," Mendel replied. "When did you get here?"

"Last night. Sit, everyone. Where is Mordecai and Ignatz?"

"Mordecai was hiding in the barn when they took us away," Ben replied. "We don't know where Ignatz went."

"May God protect them from these terrible monsters," Mr. Katz said.

"Your wife doesn't look so well," Mendel stated. He smelled a urine-like odor close by.

"We slept on the floor last night," Mr. Katz stated. "It was cold. Ruth caught a chill. I pray she doesn't have a pneumonia."

Raisel bent down and felt the woman's clammy forehead. "She has a temperature. Do you have any medicine?"

"A few tablets of aspirin," Mr. Katz replied. "I'm going to look for a doctor while there's still daylight." He stood and brushed the dirt off the seat of his pants. "Stay here and rest, everyone."

"I'll go with you," Ben said.

Raisel gave her brother a near empty hot-water bottle. "Find some water, Ben."

"*Igen.*"

* * *

Ben and Mr. Katz threaded their way through the brick factory, stopping briefly for Ben to check the time inside his pocket watch. He closed the cover and carefully placed it into his pants pocket again.

"What time is it, Ben?"

"Three o'clock."

"Does anyone know a doctor here?" the shoemaker inquired.

"We need a doctor!" Ben loudly called.

"There may be one on the other side," someone mentioned, pointing the direction.

Ben and Mr. Katz walked between a group of fanatical religious Jews who wore long black coats and round fur hats. They glanced at the two men, then resumed their prayer chants.

"Where were you arrested?" Ben asked.

"At my shop. Last night. Ruth turned on the light by mistake. We just came back from the market when the Gestapo burst through the door. Ruth got so scared she wet herself and dropped the groceries on the floor. They stole what little money I had in the cash register, and then smashed everything in the shop, including the store front window. Bastards! My poor wife managed to salvage a couple of carrots and one onion before they took us away. That's what we have to eat tonight. Carrots and onion. And there's no place to cook here."

"Fucking Nazis," Ben muttered. "They should all turn into maggots and rot in the earth."

"Careful what you say around here, Ben. My sentiments exactly, but the Hungarian army may be even worse than the Germans. Last night I spoke to a man who escaped from a ghetto like this in Munkacs. He told me he saw Hungarian soldiers beat people to death there. And rape young women and girls. We aren't in a safe place, my friend. There's not much food here. And the living arrangements are atrocious. As you can see."

"How long do you think we'll be here?"

"I'm not sure," Mr. Katz answered. "Anyone know a doctor? A train may be coming in a few days. Someone said it will take us to a labor camp."

"Do you know where?"

"No. But I hope it's better than this shithole."

"Is there a doctor in the house?" Ben shouted. "We need a doctor."

The two men noticed an elderly woman who was washing her feet with a water hose.

"There's some water," Ben said. "I'll wait until she's through."

A man called out nearby, "Who needs a doctor?"

"I do," Mr. Katz replied as he turned around and saw a tall man dressed in a tattered blue suit, wrinkled gray necktie, and a pair of shiny black wingtip shoes. The man held a satchel, and a stethoscope dangled from his neck. Mr. Katz stared at him, gazing down at his polished shoes a moment. "Thank God ... you're just the man we've been looking for."

"I believe I know you," the doctor said. "Are you Jacob Katz, the shoemaker?"

"I am."

"I thought so. I am Dr. Cornblooth. You made these shoes for me a couple years ago. Remember?"

Ben filled the water bottle nearby while the two men spoke.

Mr. Katz looked down at the doctor's shoes. They were made from soft Italian leather. A light bulb shone above his head.

"Oh, yes!" the shoemaker exclaimed. "Now I recall. You came to me when I had my shop on William Street."

"Precisely. How are you, my old friend?" Dr. Cornblooth asked.

"Considering the circumstances, I could be worse. And you?"

"Fine … but I think the shoes you made me are holding up much better than I am."

Mr. Katz smiled. The doctor managed a chuckle. Ben came over with the filled water bottle in his hand.

"Ben, this is Dr. Cornblooth. May I introduce you to my good friend and neighbor, Benjamin Weiss."

"Hello, Mr. Weiss."

"Nice to meet you, doctor."

"Likewise."

"My wife is ill. She may have a pneumonia," Mr. Katz announced.

"Take me to her. I have some medicine in my bag."

* * *

Doctor Cornblooth knelt beside Mrs. Katz and took her temperature. He removed the glass thermometer from her mouth and read it.

"What's your prognosis, doctor?" Mr. Katz inquired.

"Your wife has a high fever. And you were correct. She has pneumonia."

"*Oy vey ist mir*," the shoemaker moaned.

The doctor prepared a syringe with a small amount of penicillin. He wiped Mrs. Katz's exposed buttock with a cotton ball soaked in alcohol, and he injected the medicine. He placed a bandage on her skin, covered her buttock, and then reached into his bag, handing Mr. Katz a small bottle.

"Give her two pills every four hours. Preferably with food. If you can find any that's edible."

"All right," Mr. Katz said, offering to pay the doctor.

He waved his hand, refusing the Hungarian currency.

"I don't want your money, Katz. Main thing your wife should feel better soon."

"I'm grateful for your help. Thank you, Dr. Cornblooth."

"You're welcome. Take care everyone.

6

When Ben woke up, it was still dark outside. The squalid living conditions in the brick factory had grown much worse since he arrived five days earlier. He sat up and eyed the rigid figures resting upon the dirt floor. It spooked him. His back hurt as he tiredly put on his dress shoes and tied the laces. He stood, got his balance, and carefully stepped over the sleeping bodies, slowly making his way toward the latrine outside, a long and narrow ditch about a meter in depth, it buzzed with flies. He pulled down his pants and relieved himself while a bright beam of light cut through the dawn mist. A train approached. Daylight came soon after.

Ben steered clear of the railroad tracks, observing an oncoming locomotive. It coughed out a bluish-black smoke and pulled a dining car, two cars with sleeping compartments and seats, and a line of boxcars that stretched a good distance. The train noisily stopped. The sun emerged, reflecting off the chrome dining car. Inquisitive boys and girls ran up and gathered beside the train. A soldier yelled at them, and they ran away. Ben returned to his spot and saw that his father was gone; his mother, sister, and brother were still asleep. Mr. Katz worriedly sat beside his wife, who was coughing and reclining on her side.

"Good morning. A train just arrived."

"I heard. Good morning, Benjamin."

"How's your wife doing?"

"A little better."

"You have more pills?" he inquired, as Mrs. Katz managed to open her eyes and look his way.

"A few, but our water supply is dwindling fast."

"Have you seen my father?"

"He went up to pray about twenty minutes ago."

"I'll go see if I can find some water and bread," Ben said.

"Good."

* * *

Waiting on a lengthy line, Ben stood behind a mother cradling a pale-skinned infant boy who was crying incessantly. The young mother's dirty blouse was torn at the shoulder; her bra strap was exposed. She turned around and looked at Ben, noticing the hot-water bottle in his hand. She held out her metal cup, a tin can.

"Can you spare some water?" the mother inquired.

"Igen."

Ben filled her cup with the remaining contents. She drank, then moistened her baby's mouth by dripping some liquid from her cracked lips.

"Thank you."

"You're welcome."

She turned away from Ben, unfastened her blouse, and then breastfed her son. The baby finally stopped crying.

The line moved a little faster. Ben opened his watch and saw it was noon. He had been waiting on the line for almost three hours. Suddenly he noticed a lot of movement in the crowd. It got noisy. The disquiet in the factory prevented him from hearing the locomotive engine start up. The mother and her infant son finally reached the front of the line. She and Ben inspected the little bit of food that was left in the pot, only a grimy liquid on the bottom. The mother wrinkled her nose and grabbed a few slices of stale rye bread from the table. Ben did the same. He refilled the hot-water bottle from a hose nearby. The woman refilled her tin can, then gently placed her baby on the ground and prepared to wash him with the hose. People around them moved in a frenzy.

"What's going on?" Ben asked an elderly man before he passed.

"The train will be leaving soon. Hurry."

"Are you coming?" Ben asked the young woman who was washing her baby's behind.

"No."

* * *

Herschel and Mr. Katz helped his wife stand, as both families prepared to make their departure from the ghetto. Hanni worried herself sick for Ben, but she finished organizing their clothes and meager belongings. Raisel wrote a note for her brother and placed it on top of his clothes bundle. She secured the note with a piece of broken brick.

"Ben is gone a long time, Mendel. I'm worried what happened to him," his wife stated.

"We have to go—we can't wait any longer, Hanni."

A Hungarian soldier yelled twice, "Start moving toward the train! Move toward the train!"

Mendel recognized the soldier; the coach of the soccer team Ben had played on a few years before.

"Mr. Szalasi, it's good to see you again. I'm Mr. Weiss. Ben's father. He scored the goal for the championship. Against Budapest. Don't you remember?"

"I don't know who you are!" the soldier shouted, as he prodded Mendel with the end of his rifle. "Move, you son of a bitch."

Hanni tearfully looked up at the Hungarian soldier, and she inquired, "Our son has gone for food and water. Can we wait a little longer for him?"

"Go! Before I beat you, old woman."

Mendel held onto his wife's arm, avoiding any more eye contact with the man.

"I'm a hundred percent sure he was the coach of Ben's team," Mendel said. "Come, Hanni. Ben will catch up to us later."

As if they were pushed by a strong ocean current, Mendel, Hani, Raisel, Herschel, and Mr. and Mrs. Katz reluctantly joined the crowd that moved toward the open boxcars.

Ben cringed when he found everyone had left the temporary dwelling. *Maybe I have the wrong spot*, he said to himself, then noticed his bundle of clothes and the note on top. He quickly read it:

> Ben,
>
> We waited for you, but we had to go.
>
> See you on the train, sweetheart.
>
> Love you,
>
> Raisel

He placed the note in his pocket, and in a panic, he grabbed his bundle and rushed toward the train.

Perched like vultures on top of a raised wooden platform, Captain Manheim and Sergeant Heimlich supervised the evacuation of the brick factory ghetto.

"They're not moving fast enough, Capitan," the sergeant stated. "At this rate we'll be here all night."

"I see. *Das ist nicht gut.*" The captain shouted through a megaphone: "Everyone get into the boxcars. *Schnell!*" He lowered the megaphone. "It would please our *führer* if we shot them all right now. Hey, Heimlich?"

The sergeant laughed and crassly answered, "I could use the target practice."

"Oh, really?"

Both men lit the American cigarettes Mendel had given them; they casually blew the smoke into the air. Captain Manheim noticed that the unruly crowd had grown more reluctant to board the train. Some outright refused.

"Here—why don't you use my pistol—Heimlich."

The captain's candid suggestion caught the sergeant off-guard. Heimlich took a couple of nervous puffs, then exhaled.

"What? To shoot someone?" the blond-haired sergeant nervously asked.

"*Ja.* Let's see if you can hit the old man with the long white beard. The one in the black coat and round fur hat. He's holding the red suitcase."

"I see him. Is this a joke, *Capitan?*"

"*Nein*. It's an order," he said, handing the sergeant his semi-automatic Luger pistol.

"He looks like a rabbi to me."

"So what? Go on, Heimlich. Shoot him. I'll wager you a beer, two whiskeys, and a hundred deutsche marks if you can hit him in the head. I'll give you two tries. If you miss—you walk to Austria—agreed?"

"Agreed," the sergeant reluctantly said, sealing the bet by shaking hands with his commanding officer. "Is it loaded?"

"Of course. But take off the safety first."

The sergeant centered himself and took two deep breaths. He confidently aimed the pistol and pulled the trigger. The bullet raced for its target, making a hole in the old man's hat, and knocking it off. While the man lifted his hand up to his head, the sergeant fired a second bullet. This time it hit the mark. The orthodox Jew fell over backwards, and a pool of blood soon formed. Mayhem let loose throughout the crowd as guard dogs barked murderously. People screamed and madly rushed past the dead man to get inside the box cars.

"Excellent shot, Heimlich."

"*Danke schön, Capitan.*"

"*Bitte schön.* They're moving faster now."

The sergeant's gut wrenched as he handed the warm pistol back to his superior officer. It was the first time he had ever killed someone.

"I'm surprised you could shoot so well," the captain mentioned. "I owe you a few drinks tonight, Heimlich. Here's your money. Count it."

"*Danke*. I was one of the top three marksmen in my class at the military academy."

"Ah, that explains it."

* * *

With the replenished hot-water bottle in his hand, Ben squeezed into a boxcar and sat on his bundle of clothes. He opened his ancestral watch, faintly seeing it was five o'clock in the afternoon. He placed the watch inside his pants pocket, took a couple bites of stale bread, and anxiously waited for the train to move. It thundered. Raindrops drummed on the boxcar roof. People cried for their loved ones. Ben did also. The odor was so bad inside the car, he barely kept from vomiting. The light lessened inside as it got warmer and warmer. His clothes became soaking wet. He called again:

"Mama? Papa? Raisel? Herschel? Mr. Katz? Are you in here? It's Benjamin."

There was a brief silence inside the car.

"I am Mr. Katz," an elderly sounding gentleman replied. "Who are you?"

"Ben Weiss. You don't sound like Katz the shoemaker."

"My name is Joseph Katz. I had a butcher shop in town for many years. I'm retired now. Are you Mendel's son?"

"*Igen.*"

"I know your father. Good man, Mendel. But I've never heard of this shoemaker. I'm sorry, Ben. They must be in another car. Does your father still have the horse and wagon?" the old man inquired.

"*Igen.*"

"*Zie gesunt,* Ben. And give my regards to your father when you see him."

"I will. May God be with you, Mr. Katz."

"You as well, son."

The brick factory had been emptied, except for the dead and those too sick or crippled to stand. The army would shoot them in the morning. As the setting sun squinted through the open building, Corporal Wagner addressed Captain Manheim on top of the raised platform.

"That's everyone, *Capitan.*"

"*Gut.*"

The captain raised the megaphone and ordered the Hungarian soldiers to close and bolt the boxcar doors. He and the sergeant climbed down from the platform and schlepped their duffel bags through the garbage-strewn factory.

"It's about time we got out of this pigsty," the captain said. "I miss my wife and *kinder*. Do you have a family—Heimlich?"

"*Nein.*"

The two men pinched their noses closed while the setting sun cast their grim shadows upon the dirt floor of the factory.

"How long is it to Munich, Sergeant?" the captain asked, as they headed for the car with the sleeping compartments.

"It's about twelve hours to Mauthausen. Germany should be another three hours from there. If everything goes according to schedule."

"*Wunderbar.*"

A shrill whistle sounded, and the train's engineer waved his cap outside the window of the locomotive.

"All aboard!" a conductor yelled.

"Take the top bunk, Sergeant," Captain Manheim ordered as he set his duffel bag on the bottom mattress. "Let's go find ourselves a nice comfortable seat in the dining car. It's going to be a long and boring ride to Munich."

7

May 30, 1944

With his back pressed against the metal wall inside the boxcar, Ben felt the train suddenly move forward and roll away from the brick factory. It crept down the tracks like a gigantic iron millipede. Ben had another gulp of water before handing the container to someone beside him.

The train approached an impoverished neighborhood on the outskirts of town, where stinking garbage burned inside large, rusted barrels. Behind their clapboard homes, soot-faced gentile children happily played near the tracks; they observed the oncoming train through the dusky light. They waved and shouted to the engineer sitting high up in the locomotive; he waved back to the children, who were unaware of the human cargo riding inside the oxygen-deprived cars. The youths counted each car as it passed, until the caboose finally arrived. The train's horn blew in the distance, and the children walked home in the dark, drumming their sticks against the metal trash barrels. The Nazi locomotive engineer carefully opened a small vial, and he snorted a powdery white substance.

* * *

Ben maneuvered his cramped body and watched as a woman in the boxcar somehow managed to light two

Sabbath candles. She tearfully recited the blessing. There was light ... but only for a few minutes. A group of orthodox Jews sang a Sabbath evening prayer by heart. Ben and some others sang along with them:

Beloved, come, the bride to meet

The Sabbath Princess let us greet

For it is blessing's constant spring

Of old ordained divinely taught

Last in creation, first in thought

Beloved, come, the bride to meet

The Sabbath Princess let us greet

Arouse thyself, awake and shine

Thy light has come, the light divine

Awake and sing, and over thee

The glory of the Lord shall be

Beloved come, the bride to meet

The Sabbath Princess let us greet

Crown of thy husband, come in peace

Let joy and gladsome song increase

Among His faithful, sorrow-tried

His chosen people, come, O bride

Beloved, come, the bride to meet

The Sabbath Princess let us greet.

A child screamed on the other side of the car, and someone urinated into a wooden bucket near the center of the compartment. Ben needed to go also, but he held it in. He closed his eyes and silently prayed: *Where am I, Lord? Why do we have to suffer like this? Please help us.*"

The candles burned out.

* * *

German officers and soldiers seated themselves at tables and enjoyed the comfort of a sleek, stainless-steel dining car while their raunchy-smelling cigar and cigarette smoke thickened the air like a French chef's *roux.* Formally dressed waiters served them dinner, and the men voraciously ate plates of schnitzel, sauerkraut, peas, and potato. They washed down the food with a refreshing Hungarian spring water, Riesling wine, dark beer, whiskey, and Liebfraumilch. The train bumped along the rails, while plates, glasses, and silver chimed and rattled upon the white linen tablecloths. Bartenders and waiters nibbled on bites of food between serving duties, as a bow-tied busboy carried away the soldiers' licked-clean plates. A waiter named Otto took the men's dessert orders:

"Ice cream or fruit cocktail, *Capitan?*"

"I'll have the fruit cocktail, please," Captain Manheim replied.

"For you, Sergeant?"

"Three dark beers and two more whiskeys," he replied, slipping the waiter ten German marks. "Your service was excellent, Otto."

"*Danke schön,* Sergeant."

"*Bitte schön.*"

"Would you like a dessert, Corporal?"

"Vanilla ice cream *bitte*," he replied, peering through his inch-thick eye lenses.

Captain Manheim wiped his mouth and hands with a cloth napkin before reaching into his shirt pocket for a deck of playing cards. "Anyone up for a game of poker?"

Sergeant Heimlich smiled. "My favorite card game. *Ja, Capitan,* I'm in. Will you be joining us, Wagner?"

* * *

Loud bells that were clanging at a railroad crossing suddenly awakened Ben. A sensation of pins and needles shot through his hands, legs, and feet. He asked the person next to him, "Do you know where we are?"

"It's probably a big city," replied a man who was squinting through a hole in the boxcar's metal wall. He saw what looked like the headlights of a car. They heard trolley bells, music, and laughter.

"Budapest?" Ben asked.

"It could be."

The train slowly chugged into a station and grinded its wheels to a halt. The engine exhaled steam. From a lighted platform, a Hungarian trainman announced in a boisterous voice, "Budapest! Budapest Station!"

A cluster of German and Hungarian troops milled about the station platform, while a much larger group of prominent Hungarian Jewish families waited with their fashionable handbags and suitcases, excited to board the newly arrived train. Some of them were doctors, lawyers, teachers and professors, businessmen and women, politicians, and clergymen. Husbands and wives were accompanied by infants, children, and teenage sons and daughters. Several poorer-looking families bleakly stood nearby; their meager belongings bundled in white sheets and pillowcases. Those parents argued while their babies cried for milk or diaper changes. Ben placed his ear against the boxcar and clearly heard the infants' wails.

Although the evening wasn't a particularly cold one, the well-to-do women on the platform had dressed in fine wool skirts, mink coats, dressy leather boots, white gloves, and feathered bonnets. Their diamond jewelry sparkled in the yellow lamplight. The gentlemen wore the latest style boots and shoes, silk ties, tailored suits, and black felt top hats. They casually draped their tweed overcoats and double-breasted suit jackets over their arms and shoulders, while their young girls held dolls, and little boys excitedly gripped red rubber balls. The children and adolescents were also dressed in their Sunday best.

When the wealthy Hungarian Jews had purchased their first-class tickets, the travel agent in Budapest had told them the fare would include a full-course dinner and breakfast, plus private sleeping compartments for them and their children. The travel agent had also promised, that when the passengers reached their destination, they would be housed at ski resorts in the neutral Swiss Alps—far from the imminent dangers of war. Their lodging and meals, of course, would be paid courtesy of the German government.

The sedentary reptilian locomotive exhaled steam while the Hungarian soldiers opened the doors of three partially filled boxcars. Large black capital *A*s and *D*s had been painted on the sides of the cars. Soldiers first guided the impoverished families into the cars, filling them three-quarters full. The affluent group of Hungarians watched and felt sorry for them.

A tall, well-dressed woman on the platform argued with one of the Hungarian soldiers. In her high heels, she stood a foot taller than the soldier. He was telling the woman and her husband to board the boxcar with the capital *A* painted on it. "Get inside," the soldier ordered the affluent couple.

She showed him their tickets. "There must be some mistake," the high-heeled woman told the soldier. "I'm sure it's a mistake. My husband and I only travel in first class."

The Hungarian soldier scowled. "First class? Are you Jews out of your fucking minds? Get inside that boxcar—now!"

He stiffly pointed his finger at the opening. The high-heeled woman and her husband smelled a nasty odor coming from inside the metal compartment. The soldier pushed the woman, and she started screaming hysterically. Others watched, and they also refused to board. Her husband raised his fist, ready to strike the soldier.

"What's going on here?" asked a German soldier regarding the dispute.

"This couple won't board the train."

"And why not?" the German soldier inquired.

"They claim to have first-class tickets," the Hungarian soldier replied.

"First-class tickets?"

"*Igen.*"

In defense of his wife, the woman's husband told the Nazi, "We can't travel in that filthy cattle car. We paid good money for this trip."

"Good money? Let me see those tickets," the German soldier requested.

The wife handed them over.

"These tickets are indeed first-class, but unfortunately all the first-class seats and sleeping compartments have been reserved for military officers," the soldier explained. "*Das ist* standard protocol."

"What?" the wife asked.

"You heard me," the soldier answered, as he tore the tickets in half and threw them under the train. "Now get your pretty little asses inside that first-class boxcar. *Schnell!*"

"We're not going in there," the wife said, while crossing her arms over her broad chest. She was an imposing woman who always stood up for herself and her husband.

"Oh, no? Then you won't be going anywhere," the German soldier told her.

He took out his revolver and shot the tall woman between her eyes, then he killed her husband. The couple fell onto the platform. After hearing the loud gun shots, Ben's body suddenly jerked.

The German soldier told the Hungarian soldier, "There. Your problem is solved, comrade."

"*Igen, Capitan.*"

Both soldiers smiled, then the Hungarian quickly removed the dead man's gold wristwatch. The Nazi pulled off the woman's diamond ring and stashed it inside his pocket. He looked inside the man's wallet and pulled out a wad of American dollars. Four Hungarian soldiers came along and placed the dead couple into body bags before carrying them off the platform. The frightened crowd chaotically squeezed into the boxcars. The doors were closed, and the train sat in the station for two more hours while some mechanical repairs were made.

* * *

A rambunctious group of drunken German officers sang a patriotic song of the Fatherland as they joyfully meandered arm-in-arm along the platform. They stumbled aboard the train and noisily headed for the sleeping car.

A conductor handed the sinister-looking train engineer a steak sandwich and a bottle of whiskey. He thanked him and waved his dirty cap out the locomotive window. The conductor blew his whistle, then announced they would be leaving in two minutes. A late-arriving troop marched onto the platform and jumped onto the slowly departing train.

* * *

In the dining car, Captain Manheim ordered three more whiskeys. He shuffled a deck of cards, cut them, and then dealt. Sergeant Heimlich looked at his cards and frowned; he was quickly losing the money he had won from the captain's wager back at the brick factory. The corporal fared better, but not by much.

The soft orange glow of Budapest gradually faded, as the long iron horse disappeared into the black Slovakian countryside.

8

The morning sun came up over the Austrian Alps, dripping its tangerine light down the glistening, snow-capped heights. In a valley below the tall mountains, a serpentine river overflowed with schools of silver-speckled rainbow trout and fat Danube salmon. The deportation train Ben was on, rolled past virgin forests, but the bucolic landscape appeared more like a blotched watercolor painting to the sleepless and hungover locomotive engineer; he dozed intermittently as the railroad tracks ebbed and flowed along the winding route.

* * *

In the train's stainless-steel dining car, German high-ranking officers and soldiers had just finished breakfast, when the Vienna railway station came into focus. The groggy engineer pulled the brake lever, and the cars slowly grinded to a stop. An obsequious little conductor yelled out, "Vienna Station. Vienna, Austria!"

The doors parted, and the soldiers and officers disembarked. A new engineer came on to start his shift, relieving the other one. The old engineer staggered onto the station platform, where he was met by his irate wife, who hollered profanities at him; she slapped his head a couple times before they drove off in a dented BMW.

The conductor announced the next destination, then relaxed in the dining car, where he devoured an egg sandwich stacked with ham slices.

The train departed Vienna.

* * *

A little fresh air and light filtered through the tomb-like box car while Ben grabbed his sack of clothes and struggled his way to the piss bucket. When he reached it, he just about died from the disturbing odor. He urinated and vomited right after.

* * *

Well into the Austrian countryside, the long train passed ancient castles, farms, and sleepy villages peppered with tall white church steeples and spires. The red-shingled roof of a Jesuit monastery appeared above a steep hill, and the engineer briefly stopped at a nutshell hamlet, where three Benedictine monks were met by a blue, late model Mercedes that shuttled them to the cloistered abbey on top of the hill. The River Danube quietly ran nearby. The train chugged another fifteen kilometers down the tracks until it coasted alongside a chalk-white building, the town of Mauthausen's train station. While he squeezed his fat body through the sleeping cars, the conductor hollered: "Station Mauthausen. Wake up! Everyone off for Mauthausen."

Hung over, sleep-deprived, and penniless from the poker game they had the night before, Sergeant Heimlich and Corporal Wagner tiredly carried their duffel bags off the train while prison kapos wearing white armbands positioned wooden ramps against the boxcars. When the sergeant gave the order, soldiers unlatched the doors. Mean-spirited dogs tugged on their leashes and barked themselves into a frenzy, eagerly awaiting the fresh shipment of Jews and gentiles recently deported from Hungary, Slovakia, and Austria. Toward the rear of the train, boxcars painted with the large black capital *A*s and *D*s, remained locked; their human cargo was still sandwiched inside, struggling to breathe. Sergeant Heimlich and Corporal Wagner dropped their duffel bags into a waiting *Kübelwagen* before it drove off.

* * *

Ben wasn't sure if he was alive or not—not until the boxcar door opened and a harsh sunlight temporarily blinded him. A burst of life-giving oxygen flooded his lungs while someone's knees pressed against his back; he turned around and saw a dead man. Several others around him had also expired en route. As if he were dreaming, Ben observed their misty, etheric blue soul-bodies escape through their mouths, leave the boxcar, and then fly up into the sky. The remaining orthodox Jews in the car recited the Mourner's Kaddish, the Jewish prayer for the dead.

German soldiers loudly announced through white megaphones, "Everyone out. *Rouse!*"

Ben moved in excruciatingly painful increments; his neck, back, elbow, and knee joints cracked. He stood hunched-over, grabbed his compressed sack of clothes, and carefully descended the ramp onto a concrete platform. Ben turned his stiff neck and caught sight of an exhausted but familiar face.

"Katz! Jacob!"

The shoemaker recognized Ben's voice. He saw him waving by the car next to his. Mr. Katz raggedly approached him. And they hugged.

"You're alive—thank God—where are we?" Mr. Katz inquired.

"I don't know, but the soldiers are speaking German," Ben replied.

"After riding in that death train, anywhere is good right now," Mr. Katz stated.

"I agree."

Ben and Mr. Katz heard someone's high pitched voice below them.

"We are in Austria," replied a Hungarian Gypsy dwarf who was no taller than the height of the men's waists. "The town is called Mauthausen. I used to come here when I worked for a traveling circus."

Ben looked down at the short man. "Thank you, my friend."

"You're welcome."

"Where's your wife?" Ben asked Mr. Katz.

"Inside the boxcar. I couldn't move her. She wasn't breathing."

"Let's go back in and take her out."

"I don't know if that's possible, Benjamin."

Just then, men dressed in prison clothes shouted, "Out of our way!" and they parked large push-wagons in front of the boxcars. The prisoners climbed into the wretched-smelling compartments and carried out the lifeless passengers one by one; they loaded them into the push-wagons before carting them away.

"There's my wife," Mr. Katz announced, as he noticed her on the top of some other bodies inside a push-wagon. "I will follow them to see if I can bury her," he said.

"Don't," Ben warned.

"Get back in line, Jew!" a soldier yelled, striking Mr. Katz's upper leg with a baton.

He cried out in pain.

"Be careful, Mr. Katz—there's nothing we can do about it now," Ben said.

"Poor Ruth," he lamented.

"I know. I wonder what happened to the rest of my family," Ben said.

"They were put into a boxcar toward the rear of the train. I wanted to go with them, but the soldiers refused."

Able to speak fluent German, Ben timidly asked a blond-haired soldier, "Pardon me."

"*Ja?*"

"Are we going to a labor camp?" Ben inquired.

The soldier smiled and nudged a soldier beside him.

"*Nein, tateleh,*" the German soldier replied. "There aren't any labor camps here. Only a concentration camp farther up the road."

"I don't know what that is," Ben stated.

The soldier explained, "A concentration camp is similar to a fine resort hotel. You'll enjoy a lovely private suite, a health spa, and a restaurant that serves three gourmet meals a day. The camp even has a tennis court, a golf course, and a heated swimming pool. You will have such a good time there—I envy you."

In between sucking on their cigarettes, both of the soldiers laughed. One of them made a sound from the back of his throat; he spit a globule of mucus on the ground. Ben looked up at the soldier, knowing what he had told him could not be true.

"And where did you learn how to speak such proper German?" one of the soldiers asked Ben.

"At my school in Hungary. Will this be the last stop on the train line?"

"*Nein, tateleh,*" the soldier affectionately replied. "From here, the train will go on to other wonderful vacation resorts. Like Auschwitz, Dachau, Bergen-Belsen and Treblinka."

"Oh . . . *danke schön,*" Ben said to the soldier.

"*Bitte schön, tateleh.*"

The two soldiers laughed again, while the air got heavy with a dead-animal smell coming from the woods beyond the railroad tracks. One of them noticed the odor, wrinkling his face. He remarked, "Dead dog."

"*Ja.*"

"Form a line and march!" another soldier screamed through a megaphone.

Ben, Mr. Katz, and the others unsteadily foot-slogged down the train platform and onto Mauthausen's main street. Women on their hands and knees fearfully glanced up at the newly arrived group. A woman kapo shouted at them, and they resumed scrubbing the sidewalk with brushes and pails of soapy water.

"Keep marching!" a Hungarian kapo yelled at Ben's group. "Eyes front."

If the parade wasn't moving fast enough, soldiers and kapos hit them with sticks and wooden batons. The deportees trudged past several townsfolk who appeared to be frozen in time. When the kapos or soldiers weren't looking, a few of the courageous and sympathetic locals dropped fruit, sandwiches, or lit cigarettes on the road, for the men and women exiles lucky enough to pick it up.

The thousand or more exiles came to the outskirts of town, where they scaled a steep hill which led them to a gravel drive. An imposing granite wall appeared. Above the entrance, the insignia of a large dark eagle and swastika was held in place with iron bars. Before Ben and Mr. Katz passed through the prison's stone gate— they silently read a posted sign written in German: Wilkommen zu Konzentrationslager Mauthausen. Welcome to Mauthausen Concentration Camp.

9

Back at the Mauthausen train station, the fat little conductor hurriedly waddled alongside the same train that Ben and Mr. Katz had disembarked earlier. The conductor announced the next stop, then clambered aboard. He sat in the dining room, drank an espresso, and then finished the other half of his pastrami sandwich on pumpernickel bread.

At noon, the train departed the chalk-white station, leaving behind the Gypsy women scrubbing the station platform on their hands and knees. The innocent little village of Mauthausen faded from view, as well as the pink and blue wildflowers that swayed alongside the tracks.

Now that many of the boxcars carried much less weight, the train moved faster.

Three hours had gone by, and Captain Manheim carried his duffel bag off the train at a bustling Munich station, where he was warmly greeted by his wife and two young children.

The fat little conductor shouted through a window, "Next stop, Dachau!"

Men and women in the beer halls of Munich celebrated and cheered as the deportation train passed through their city. It soon arrived in a more country-like place enclosed by barbed-wire fences and guard towers. The Dachau concentration camp appeared. The train stopped. The boxcars with the capital *D*s were opened, and the wealthy and poor occupants stiffly climbed down from the freight containers and were taken inside the camp.

The aged, crippled, and mothers with infants and young children were sent directly to the gas chambers while a select group of children were brought to a brick building, where doctors would perform cruel and bizarre medical experiments on them. Other groups of men, women, criminals, homosexuals, and political dissidents who were not taken to the gas chambers, were ordered to strip naked. Their shoes, fur coats, hats, suits, dresses, bras and girdles, wigs, eyeglasses, artificial limbs, canes, jewelry, wallets, and toys were all placed in individual piles, and later recycled by camp prisoners. In separate groups, the naked men and women were lined up shoulder to shoulder against a backdrop of lofty pine trees.

After what seemed like an eternity, the men in the Nazi firing squads stared down their gun barrels at the undressed prisoners. While they waited for their orders to shoot, a few in the firing squads must have thought: Do I not have a conscience? How will I live with this? I dare not tell my wife or children. I'm just following orders. If I refuse to kill, I'll be charged with insubordination. *I'm just following orders.*

Horrified, the group of unclothed women shielded their pubic areas and breasts, while the group of blank-eyed men bashfully covered their penises. Some did not. Commands were given. And the firing squads pulled their triggers. Loud cracks rang out for several moments as a hailstorm of bullets flew through the air. The victims fell. A few minutes later, several haggard prisoners from Dachau loaded the dead men and women into wagons and trucks, then hauled them off to the crematory. Tractors and bulldozers shoveled the remaining corpses into mass graves, which were dug in a field behind the prisoners' barracks.

* * *

The train that originated from Beregszász left Dachau, traveled north, and soon crossed into German-occupied Poland, where it made a final stop at the infamous Auschwitz concentration camp. The tracks led the train a few meters from the camp's entrance, where kapos and Polish and German soldiers wrenched open the boxcar doors. The dead and the living watched with bleak, frigid eyes. It was a cool summer day, yet the sun shined brightly.

Dressed in striped, ill-fitting uniforms, children curiously observed from behind a barbed-wire fence as another shipment of exiles was unloaded. Moments later, another train pulled into the camp. And one after that. The freight trains arrived continuously, day and night. They brought more Jews and gentiles from Hungary. Other trains came from big Polish cities like Warsaw and Krakow, or the impoverished Jewish shtetls in the bleak countryside of Poland, Ukraine, Czechoslovakia, Belarus, Lithuania, and Latvia.

Barely alive themselves, Mendel, Hanni, Herschel, and Raisel wearily tottered along the Auschwitz train platform. It was extremely crowded. Looks of fear, shock, or confusion covered the face of most every person who disembarked the trains. Like Mendel and his family, several carried sheets or pillowcases stuffed with belongings; others held suitcases.

"I hope Ben is here," Hanni told her husband.

Mendel remained silent. He coughed into a dirty handkerchief, almost fainting from a horrible odor in the air.

"What's that smell, daddy?" Herschel asked.

"I don't know, son. Smoke from a factory maybe."

Herschel started to cry. Raisel comforted her brother by wrapping her arms around him. "It's all right, Herschel."

"I want to go home, Raisel—the chickens are hungry."

"We will, Herschel—don't worry."

Polish soldiers and kapos ordered everyone to move along the train platform, join lines, and march.

Mendel and his wife, son, and daughter approached an iron gate with large German words welded onto an ornamental sign high above.

"What does that mean, Mendel?" Hanni asked.

"It's German . . . for work will set you free."

"Work will set you free?"

"*Igen*, sweetheart. "

Dressed in white lab coats and gloves, male and female doctors examined the camp's newcomers one by one. Hanni reached the front of her line, and a German doctor placed a stethoscope onto her chest, briefly listening to her strong but nervous heartbeat. The doctor grimaced and pointed her toward a group of crippled and elderly women, mothers with babies and small children.

The doctor examined Raisel next. After asking her a few questions, the examiner quickly motioned Raisel to join a group of healthy young women and older girls.

* * *

Mendel and Herschel stood at the front of their line. A male physician in a white lab coat marked something on a clipboard, then focused his blue, wolf-like eyes on Mendel.

"How old are you?"

"Forty-eight and a half," Mendel replied in German.

"Do a deep knee-bend for me."

Mendel succeeded, but struggled, as he pushed himself up. He was dehydrated from the horrendous journey. The doctor gave him a disparaging glance, placing a stethoscope onto his chest. Mendel stared at a group of strong and healthy men, hoping that Ben might be with them. The doctor removed the medical instrument.

"Look at me," he sternly said. "Do you smoke cigarettes?"

"On occasion."

"Not a healthy habit."

"I know. My wife wants me to quit."

"Don't worry—you will soon. You're not suitable for the work here. It will be too difficult for you."

"But I can try, no?"

"*Nei!*" the doctor shouted in Polish. He ordered Mendel to join a large group of puny boys and elderly and crippled old men. One man sat crying in a wheelchair.

Herschel stepped forward next. He dared not look at the doctor's face, only glancing at his high black boots.

"Is he your *fater*?" the doctor asked him. "Look at me!"

"*Igen*," Herschel meekly replied.

"Age?"

"Eighteen."

"You look younger," the doctor said. "Make a fist and bend your arm."

The doctor felt Herschel's weakened bicep muscle, and he told him to join the group his father was in.

After the selection process ended, male and female kapos led the groups to their next destination.

* * *

Inside a cold, damp building, female guards ordered Raisel and her group to remove their foul-smelling clothing. She took off her favorite dress, underwear, and the pair of red high heels Mr. Katz had made her. Except for shoes, women inmates gathered the clothing into push wagons and burned it in piles outside in an empty field. Raisel and her group took freezing cold showers, then stood soaking wet, on a concrete floor in a drafty room. A few female prisoners sprayed the new group for lice before they were given dismal, pajama-like uniforms, and stiff wooden clogs. The female inmates quickly dressed, then sat on benches, where skin-headed barbers cut their long and short locks and shaved their heads bald. Afterward, the women and teenage girls were brought across the room and seated at a long table, where tattoo artists inscribed a blue, six-digit serial number onto each one's forearm; they were officially registered as prisoners of Auschwitz. Two female kapos brought Raisel and her group out into the septic air and marched them to a row of wood barracks.

* * *

Basking in the afternoon sunshine, two Nazi officers practiced hitting golf balls on a grassy field beyond a tall barbed-wire fence. Previously, a diesel-powered bulldozer had hollowed out a deep, rectangular pit in the field they played in. Tractors pushed skin-and-bone corpses into the long grave. The tractors drove off while the powerful earth mover dug another hole nearby. One of the German officers barked, "Fore!" as he swung a nine iron. The club made contact, and the ball soared high and fell into the gaping crater the earth mover had dug.

"Excellent shot, Klaus."

"*Danke.*"

"You know, Klaus, I'm anxious to get back to Aachen. I really miss the golf course in my hometown. You must come and visit my family and I—after we—win the war, that is. We shall play a proper eighteen holes and have beers and thick juicy steaks in the backyard barbecue. How does that sound, Klaus?"

"I would enjoy that very much, Lieutenant."

"*Wunderbar.*"

The other officer placed his ball on a tee, swung his club, and then hit a line-drive shot that swerved downward and ricocheted off the departing bulldozer in the distance. The little ball swiftly rolled toward the large rectangular hole and dropped into the open mouth of a dead person.

"Nice swing, Gunther, but I would have to say that's interference. Why don't you try again."

* * *

On the other side of the tall barbed-wire fence, Hanni and the group she was in straggled along a dusty path. The afternoon sun glared down on them as she lagged a few moments to admire some pretty iris flowers someone had planted for a border along the fence. She inhaled a ghastly smell while picking one of the flowers.

"Keep moving," a female Polish guard hollered.

Hanni's group of elderly women, mothers cradling babies, and young children, approached a long structure, where twelve chimney stacks billowed out a stinking white smoke. Ashes fell upon them as they hobbled to another building. On that one, the German word *duschraum*, was written above two metal doors. The kapos ordered the women and children to strip naked and form a line outside the building. They handed them chunks of soap and small boxes to deposit their jewelry, money, and eyeglasses.

Hanni overheard two elderly Hungarian women in front of her.

"This place frightens me, Ethel," Miriam, the shorter woman said.

"What are you so afraid of, sister?"

"Everything," Miriam answered. "Why did we have to come to Poland? We should have stayed in Budapest. It's freezing here."

"We had no choice," the bigger sister explained. "The Hungarian army would have killed us in Budapest."

"We could have hidden in the attic—I miss my cat, Ethel."

"She'll be fine. Mrs. Bonhoeffer said she'll take good care of her while we're away."

"We're not going back to Hungary, sister. And I'll never see my cat again."

"Oh, please, don't talk like that Miriam."

"Why? It's true. I wish we had wings so we could fly away from here. I don't want to take a shower, Ethel."

Hanni followed behind the two sisters, as they moved closer to the *duschraum* entrance.

"We'll smell like boar hogs if we don't wash ourselves, Miriam."

"I don't give a rat's ass. These Nazi bastards can go fuck themselves, as far as I'm concerned."

"Miriam, please . . . they will hear you."

Just then, one of the Hungarian kapos approached the line with a hard stick in her hand.

"Move along, ladies," the Hungarian kapo urged. "Place your things in the box you received. They'll be returned to you later. After you clean yourselves, you'll get new clothes, and everyone will enjoy coffee and cake in the dining hall. Hurry up now."

An elderly woman asked, while another kapo handed her a small chunk of soap, "Where are the towels and bathrobes?"

"Don't worry, grandma. I'll bring them to you. Go inside."

Before the two sisters in front of Hanni reached the shower room entrance, they moved off the line and whispered to each other.

The woman kapo approached the sisters, and she asked them in Hungarian, "Why aren't you going inside the shower room?"

Ethel, the taller woman, replied, "My sister doesn't feel well. If she isn't going in, I'm not either."

With a look of astonishment, the kapo exclaimed, "Both of you must take a shower. Go inside. Now!"

"I don't believe this is a shower room," the shorter sister said.

"Don't talk back, bitch!"

The kapo raised her hard stick and whacked Miriam's frail arm. A red bruise appeared.

"I said go in!"

"You hurt me."

She started crying, and her taller sister stepped between her and the kapo.

"Don't you ever hit my sister again—you fat douchebag!"

The kapo raised her baton, about to strike Ethel, when she grabbed it and walloped the kapo's jaw so hard it fractured, leaving her unconscious on the ground a few moments.

A female guard came over and asked the kapo, who was holding her bloody mouth. "Why are you lying down? Get those prisoners inside the shower room. *Rouse!*"

"That woman hit me with my baton," the kapo cried, pointing to the taller sister. "I think she broke my jaw."

After Hanni witnessed the brawl, she rapidly entered the *duschraum.* Moments later, she heard two gunshots fired outside. The group was packed into the bath house; its metal doors were slammed shut and locked from the outside. Desperate echoes reverberated inside the queasy blue chamber; an anemic yellow light bulb glowed from the ceiling. Hanni and the others stood under the showerheads and turned the faucets. Nothing came out. From a small cubicle connected to the *duschraum,* a male guard looked through a glass peephole in a wall, and he lecherously observed the naked and frightened women, girls, and babies. As the guard espied the occupants, he fondled his privates. He opened the pressure on a valve, and a poison gas choked Hanni and the others in the jam-packed chamber. Inmates who were working outside heard the desperate screams within the *duschraum.* They turned their heads and kept working.

Mendel and Herschel entered the men's shower room at Auschwitz. It was also illuminated by an eerie yellow light on the ceiling. They could hardly move inside; the chamber was so crowded. Mendel took off his top hat and affectionately brushed the felt material before hanging it on a hook. Too ashamed to look at his father's nakedness, Herschel began to cry. His father comforted him by putting a hand on his son's trembling shoulder.

"I'm scared something terrible is going to happen to us, Papa," Herschel said.

"Me too, son. Me too."

No water came out of the shower heads there either. A guard released the poison Zyklon gas and Mendel, Herschel, and the others experienced a burning inside their nose, throat, and lungs. Some men banged their heads against the hard floor. Others pulled their hair out and screamed. Some pounded and kicked and scratched the locked metal doors until their knuckles and feet became bruised and bloody. The queasy blue walls spun around in a fiery circle. Mendel felt as if his skin was burning from the inside out.

Everything stopped. And there was an unending silence in Auschwitz. The bodies inside the *duschraum* quietly rested on the cold floor. Their souls had escaped the gas chamber via the vent holes the poison gas had come through. *Heavenly hosts* met the rising spirits, and they helped them make their departure from the camp.

The kapos reluctantly unlocked and opened the *duschraum* doors. They peered inside while a final glimmer of daylight peacefully landed upon the naked corpses.

10

June 1, 1944

Inside one of the Hungarian barracks at Mauthausen, a guard pointed his flashlight at Ben's face while a mean Lithuanian kapo bashed a hard stick against the prisoners' bedposts. Ben's eyelids snapped open like a sudden pull and release on a venetian blind. Mr. Katz awoke in the bed underneath. The guard and the kapo moved on to the next section of bunks.

"Rise and shine, scumbags!" one of them yelled in Hungarian.

Ben sat up and silently recited a Hebrew prayer said upon awakening: the *Modeh Ani.* "I offer thanks to You, my living God and eternal King, for You have mercifully restored my soul within me. Your faithfulness is great."

Ben and Mr. Katz climbed down from the bunk bed and put on their flimsy canvas shoes. They used the primitive latrine inside the barracks. Afterward, they trudged to the communal washroom and splashed cold water onto their faces from a big round sink. Other prisoners elbowed for position behind, as a sedentary dawn appeared from a large wood-framed window there.

"Let's see what's on the breakfast menu, Ben," the shoemaker quipped while he wiped some water from his nose.

The two men retrieved their metal bowls, cups, and utensils, then stood on a line and waited until the kitchen kapos served them a cold mush and a bitter chicory coffee. They carried their breakfast to the long dining table, where several other Hungarian men were sitting. Ben and Mr. Katz had barely swallowed two bites when the mean Lithuanian kapo shouted, "Hurry up and finish eating. Wash up and go outside for roll call. Now!"

A few men at the table laughed as Ben regurgitated his slop after gunning down the muddy coffee. Everyone stood and headed for the kitchen sinks, where they washed their bowls, cups, and utensils, and then stored them in numbered lockers. The prisoners gathered for roll call outside in the spacious garage yard.

While Ben waited for his name to be called, he closed his eyes a few moments, and his mother and father appeared to him in a vision. He saw them riding on the horse-drawn wagon. A wreath of red roses adorned the horse's neck. The body of his younger brother, Herschel, rested inside a coffin on the wagon. His mama and papa wore ghostly white shrouds. Hanni had on her flowery yellow apron; her face was gone; she held the flower she had picked in Auschwitz. Mendel put on his black top hat; he gripped the reins and smiled at Ben. A mysterious purple light glowed around them, and their voices spoke through the foggy morning air:

Goal!

You want a ride home with us, Benjamin?

Give the horse an apple, son.

Wash up for supper, Ben.

How come you haven't milked the cow yet?

We're having stuffed cabbage tonight.

Pearl wants to go to America, Mendel.

And I suppose all the streets there are paved with gold?

Where is Newburgh, Hanni?

The voices stopped and the vision disappeared. Ben opened his eyes to the brackish morning sky and the disheveled prisoners grouped around him.

A guard yelled, "Benjamin Weiss!"

"Present," he answered, waving his striped cap in the air.

"You're working in the quarry today," the guard shouted.

Ben nodded and covered his shaved head. He joined Mr. Katz, who stood in a work crew forming nearby.

The guard called the next name on the roster.

"Applebaum!"

"Here."

* * *

Flanked by guards and kapos who were accompanied by vicious German shepherds and rottweilers, Ben and his work crew of almost a hundred left the garage yard and marched down the gravel road about a kilometer until the Wiener Graben rock quarry appeared. At the far edge of the worksite, Ben smelled a fragrant odor coming from an evergreen forest nearby. Everyone stopped to urinate as the morning sun trickled over the forest behind the quarry. Huge white boulders and jagged rocks formed a stark terrain. Ben remained at the spot while the others sluggishly departed. He watched a flock of black kites and brown buzzards fly overhead. They called to him, speaking in a strange kind of language he seemed to understand.

"You poor pathetic human being. How foolish of you to come here. We fly over this place daily, and watch hundreds perish from the hard labor. Mr. Weiss. You as well shall not survive this hell for long."

Ben stood next to a tree and urinated, suddenly realizing that everyone had moved on toward the granite quarry. The birds circled the horizon and once more hovered above his head. Again, they spoke: "In the end, your oppressors will turn you into a walking skeleton, and when your body is put in the ground, the worms here will have little to eat of you."

One of the birds crapped on Ben's shoulder, and he angrily stared up as the flock flew off.

"Hey! What are you doing over there, muscleman?" a guard yelled from a short distance away. He pointed a rifle with a sharp bayonet on the end of it. "Get moving, Jew."

Ben hurried to catch up with the others, passing a stagnant pond with a scummy green surface. The water appeared to be hot and polluted. He suddenly flashed back to what the Nazi soldier had told him when he arrived at Mauthausen. *It even has a heated swimming pool, a tennis court, a golf course, and three gourmet meals a day.* Ben brushed away the thought and caught up with his work detail on the bottom of the quarry, at the base of a steep hill. A stone staircase was built into a high mound. Another work crew was already climbing up the 186 rock steps to the top. Each laborer carried a heavy granite stone in a wooden carrier on their back. The multitude of men struggled like pack-mules up the perilous incline. Ben watched them from below.

"There you are—I've been looking for you," Mr. Katz told Ben. "Hurry. Put on a carrier. I'll load your block. Then you can load mine."

Ben strapped on his wood-framed backpack, and Mr. Katz uneasily placed a heavy granite block inside. Ben lowered one into his partner's carrier, and the crowded work crew soon started scaling the steps. At the top, they followed a rutted road that led them to the Danube River. There, they loaded the granite stones onto long barges. Ben and the other prisoners trudged back to the starting point at the bottom of the rock staircase. They replenished their carriers with stone, then started the arduous routine all over again.

As they labored under the scorching midday sun, Ben's work detail at the quarry had decreased to about half. Many died from sunstroke and dehydration. Some of the guards had pushed workers off the top of the staircase. They would fall through the air, land on the hard rock floor below, and fracture their skeletons.

By seven o'clock that day, the sun lowered beneath the stone horizon, and the kapos' loud calls reverberated inside the quarry. "Work is finished! Everyone back to camp! Work is finished. Everyone back to camp. Work is finished . . ."

Ben took hold of Mr. Katz's arm and helped him hobble out of the quarry. They passed the stagnant pond, evergreen trees, and then trudged along the gravel road. When everyone reached the garage yard, they lined up for roll call. The dusky sky turned into a rotten mushroom blue, then black. The stars came out. Mr. Katz waited until Ben's name was called. Together, they limped back to Barracks 20.

"I'm dead tired, Ben."

"Me too."

"I don't know how I'll ever survive this work," Mr. Katz stated. "Every muscle in my body hurts."

"Mine too. We'll get some food soon. Then rest after."

"*Igen.*"

"Let's go—we're almost there," Ben said.

Ben and Mr. Katz walked between several rows of long green buildings built from wood. They found Barracks 20, what they now called home. Dangling light bulbs shone through its spooky, white-framed windows. A brown door opened and closed as each dog-tired prisoner entered. The interior was furnished with numerous three-tiered sleeping bunks and two long benches on either side of a long dining table. By the entrance, two plain chairs had been reserved for a guard and a kapo. The kitchen was located at the far end of the barracks. A communal latrine and a washroom supplied cold running water on the other side. Ben and Mr. Katz followed the other prisoners inside.

"I'm going to the latrine," Ben said. "Save me a place next to you."

"*Igen.*"

Mr. Katz opened his wooden locker and retrieved his metal bowl, cup, fork, and spoon. When he reached the front of the food line, a man plopped a tablespoon of rice into his bowl, while another kitchen kapo ladled in a watered-down soup. A haggard-looking potato peel floated on the top. Mr. Katz stared at it while he was handed a clump of hard black bread. He found himself a seat at the dinner table, squeezing beside a lanky gentleman who wore tidy gray work clothes; his narrow face was clean-shaven, his jet-black hair was grown out, unlike many of the other prisoners there. Mr. Katz braved a taste of food.

"How is it?" Ben asked as he placed his tray on the table; he sat between the shoemaker and the lanky gentleman with the slicked black hair.

"Nothing to write home about—tell you that much— but thank God we have something to eat. It's quite an improvement over the brick factory."

"*Igen*. Thanks to the almighty," Ben said. He lowered his head and closed his eyes a moment. He picked up the hard bread and knocked it against the table, sounding as if a carpenter was hammering on wood. The other men stopped chewing and looked up. They noticed Ben's sharp face and muscular upper body, a stark contrast to their gaunt frames.

Mr. Katz whispered, "Everyone's looking at us, Ben. Maybe you shouldn't knock your bread on the table like that."

Ben cleared his throat and addressed the men, "Sorry if I disturbed you."

They acknowledged his apology with grunts and nods. One man smiled, while the rest put their heads down and continued eating. The lanky man seated next to Ben took hold of his hard portion of bread and banged it against the table. He teased the other diners with a dropped jaw, open mouth, and gold front tooth. They burst out laughing. A few of the men knocked their rolls against the table. And for the time being, the somber atmosphere in the barracks had been lifted. The lanky man nudged Ben's side with his elbow and spoke to him in a city-like Hungarian:

"Put your bread in your soup, man. It will soften and be easier for you to eat."

"Oh, thanks."

"You're welcome."

Ben placed the bread in his bowl and spooned the warm yellowish liquid over it.

"My name is Zugreb. Zohar Zugreb," said the tall man with the clean-shaven countenance.

"Benjamin Weiss. And this is my good friend and neighbor. Jacob Katz."

The men shook hands with their new friend.

"Pleasure meeting you both," Zohar said. "You're new. Where do you come from?"

"Beregszász, Hungary," Ben replied. "Both of us."

"We are neighbors," Zohar stated. "My hometown is Budapest—have you been there?"

"I have."

"Never," Mr. Katz replied.

Ben ate a spoonful of soup, then paddled around the soaking bread.

"Where you working?" Zohar inquired.

"At the quarry," Ben replied. "Both of us."

"That's brutal work, my friend. Last week the guards pushed eight Dutchmen off the top of the quarry. They killed them all."

"Why?" Mr. Katz inquired.

"Because they're cruel Nazis. What else? Maybe they weren't working hard enough. I liked the Dutchmen. I can speak their language. Nice group of people. Friendly. Educated. Decent men. Teachers, doctors, and lawyers. I doubt they were used to hard labor," Zohar said, wiping away some tears.

"Oh," Ben said. "I'm sorry you lost your friends."

"I know how difficult the work is at the quarry," Zohar stated. "I worked there the first two days I was here. I hated it. My third day, the commandant came to the barracks and asked if anyone knew how to do electrical work. I'm a master electrician, so I volunteered. I've been doing that work ever since, thanks God. I would have been dead a long time if I kept working at the quarry. Better you get jobs somewhere else."

"How long have you been in Mauthausen?" Ben inquired.

"Tomorrow will be my one-year anniversary. Do either of you have a trade?"

"I was an apprentice glazier in Hungary," Ben replied. "Almost a journeyman."

"That's a very good occupation," Zohar stated. "Not many men know how to cut glass. What is your trade, Mr. Katz?"

"I'm a shoemaker."

"And he's an excellent one at that," Ben added.

"You should put those skills to work here," the electrician spoke. "There's no glazier in the camp right now. I have to do some repairs in the guards' living quarters tomorrow. I'll tell the commandant's assistant I know someone who can fix broken windows."

"That's very kind of you," Ben said.

"Can you pull some strings for me?" Mr. Katz shyly asked.

Zohar finished his last spoonful of soup and tore off a piece of his softened bread. He turned to the shoemaker. "I'm sure there are plenty of Nazi boots around here that need repairing. I'll put in a good word for you also."

"I appreciate that, Mister Zugreb."

"Please. Call me Zohar. We are friends now."

"Are you Jewish?" Ben asked him.

"No, I'm a Protestant. The mother fucking Nazis hate us too."

The Lithuanian kapo beat his stick against the dining table. He yelled, "Supper time is over, cock suckers! Get your stinking asses out of here. Wash your plates. Go take showers. Now!"

"We have to leave," Zohar said. "Watch out for that kapo. He's a cruel son of a bitch. Don't trust him for one minute. He would rat on his mother for an extra cigarette. Goodnight, gentlemen. We can talk tomorrow at supper. Save me a place by you at the table."

"We will. Good night, Zohar," Ben said.

* * *

After Ben showered for five minutes, then let the sticky air dry him, he climbed up to a top bunk, hung his hand-washed socks from the bedpost, and settled his exhausted body on a mattress of thinly layered straw.

"Did you get enough to eat, Benjamin?" Mr. Katz asked from the middle bunk.

"Yes, but I wish I had gone back for seconds. The roast beef and mashed potatoes looked delicious."

"Funny . . ."

A tiny bug gnawed at Ben's neck. "Something just bit me," he announced.

"You probably have lice," said the prisoner in the bottom bunk.

"Oh?" Ben asked.

"*Igen*. There's been an infestation of it recently," Ben's Hungarian neighbor replied. "If the fucking bastards don't delouse us more often—the creatures eat us up alive."

When another inmate heard the unsavory talk, he joined in, "Hey, muscleman. You know what we say around the camp?"

"Oh?" Ben asked.

"The lice here eat better than we do. Go to sleep. You won't feel them biting you as much."

The men laughed, and the Lithuanian kapo smashed his hard stick against Ben's bedpost. A guard hit a switch on the wall and the barracks turned pitch dark, aside for the guard's flashlight.

"Quiet! Lights out."

Ben took his pocket watch from under the mattress, gently placed it against his heart and felt the ticking. He slept.

11

The man in charge of Mauthausen, Commandant Graben, splashed through a puddle formed by an early morning sun-shower at the camp. Before he entered the officers' dining room, the five-foot eleven-inch brown-haired and brown-eyed Austrian took a rag and wiped the water off his tall Nazi boots. He glanced at the partially clouded sky, observing a broad and vibrantly colored rainbow. He went inside, poured himself a coffee, and then brought it over to his usual table by a window that had a pane missing. A woman approached his table and briefly looked out the window.

"Pretty, isn't it?" a thirty-year-old curvaceous redhead remarked while gazing at the sky. She wore a low-cut navy-blue V-neck sweater that complemented her grandiose breasts and red-freckled cleavage. She set her breakfast tray opposite the commandant.

"It is pretty. Good morning, Mrs. Holstein," the commandant greeted his secretary while wiping some cream off his square brown mustache.

"Not eating?" she asked the commandant.

"Don't have an appetite. My ulcers are bothering me this morning."

"Sorry to hear," Mrs. Holstein said.

The commandant enviously eyed the flirtatious woman's eggs Benedict, rye toast, hash browns, four strips of bacon cooked crisp, and two sausage links. "See you're eating a healthy breakfast this morning," he stated.

"I'm skipping lunch today," she said, draping a cloth napkin across her pleated black skirt; she wore no panties underneath it. A gaudy pair of fourteen-karat gold earrings dangled from her earlobes, a birthday present given to her by an admiring guard at the camp; the jewelry once belonged to a Jewish countess from Romania, who'd been stripped of it before dying in the gas chamber at Hartheim Castle.

The secretary bit into her toast while the commandant secretly observed the hollow between her breasts. Her aqua-blue eyes shimmered in the morning light. The tall German formed an erection under the table as his secretary smiled at him. She chomped on a sausage, and then generously salted and attacked one of her eggs.

Corporal Wagner opened the door to the dining room, letting in a late spring breeze. The imprudent Mrs. Holstein felt the draft waft between her pale, fleshy thighs. She crossed her legs. The corporal closed the door and noticed the provocatively dressed secretary at the table by the broken window. He poured a cup of coffee and filled a bowl with oatmeal from the steaming hot buffet table. The corporal's vision blurred some as his coke-bottle eyeglasses fogged up a few moments.

"How's your mother doing these days?" the secretary asked the commandant.

"She's well, thanks. Somewhat bored in Berlin. She's unable to get out much since the bombing started. I'm planning a visit in a month or so . . . depending on how the war goes."

"Is she safe in Berlin?"

"There's a bomb shelter in the basement of her building."

"That's good."

"Well, I won't get much work done if I stay around here," the commandant said. "That reminds me, Mrs. Holstein. I'd like you to type a letter today. My mother has a difficult time reading my handwriting."

"I know," the secretary said, grinning. She salted, then forked her other egg.

Corporal Wagner greeted them at the table. "Good morning, Commandant. Mrs. Holstein. Mind if I join you?"

"Morning, Corporal," the commandant said, detecting an offensive odor coming from the other man's direction. "See you're back from Hungary. I'm leaving, but I'm sure that Mrs. Holstein would enjoy your company."

Don 't be so sure of that, commandant, the woman thought as she caught a whiff of the corporal's well-ripened body odor.

The commandant picked up his brief case and left the table.

The alluring secretary gave the young corporal an uninterested stare as she uncrossed her legs, pushed away her half-eaten breakfast, and then removed a cigarette and a lighter from her fashionable Parisian handbag. The corporal sat beside her. She lit a cigarette and blew the smoke past his pudgy red nose. He snuck a glance of the woman's freckled cleavage.

"It's good to see you again, Mrs. Holstein," the corporal said. "How've you been?"

"Fine, thank you. But you need a bath. You stink."

"I'm sorry. I had a long train ride. I'll get one after I eat."

"Please do," the secretary said as she got up from the table and quickly squashed her cigarette in an ash tray. "Have a good day, Mr. Wagner."

"*Danke . . .* you as well."

* * *

On his way to the administration building, the commandant removed a pretty dandelion weed that grew along the sidewalk. He stashed the flower inside his shirt pocket, opened a door, and then marched down a hallway that was littered with portraits of himself and Führer Klaus von Hellmenz. He paused to straighten one of the frames before going inside his office. The commandant set his briefcase on a desk and opened the venetian blinds; a ray of light landed on an oak shelf, where two potted philodendrons and a fish aquarium sat. He fed the fish, watered the plants, and then heard a knock on the door.

"Enter."

Sergeant Heimlich appeared, greeting his superior officer with an arm raised high in a starched Nazi salute.

"*Heil Hellmenz*, Commandant."

The commandant wrinkled his nose as if he had just smelled a dead rat inside the room.

"*Ya . . . heil Hellmenz,* Heimlich. What the fuck. Lower your arm already. You haven't bathed this morning?"

"Not yet. I just came from the train station. And I ran out of cologne while I was in Hungary. Not to mention the hotel we were staying at only had freezing cold water."

"You smell, Sergeant."

"Sorry."

"How was your trip, sweetheart?" the commandant asked his lover.

"Exhausting—but productive."

"*Gut.* I presume the deportation proceedings went well?" the commandant asked, reaching into his pocket, and pulling out the dandelion. He placed the flower in a small, water-filled vase.

"Like clockwork. Would you like to hear the statistics?"

"Please . . ."

The commandant sat at his desk and smoked an American cigarette from a pack Corporal Wagner had given him in the dining room.

The blond and blue-eyed Austrian unfolded a paper and read from it:

"Two transport trains delivered twelve hundred Hungarian Jews, sixty-five Gypsies, fifty-two Jehovah's Witnesses, twelve Seventh-Day Adventists, thirty Russian officers, five American airmen, eleven Canadian airmen, fifteen British soldiers, eighteen Negroes, sixteen homosexuals, twenty-five non-Jewish political dissidents, a family of midgets, and fifty young and attractive Hungarian women for the brothel. Wealthy ladies from Budapest."

The sergeant stood there and proudly gloated.

"Excellent job, Heimlich."

"*Danke schön.*"

"You'll be sure to work them until they're skin and bones. And send the sick and crippled straight to the gas chambers. *Gut?*"

"*Yahvol.*"

"It's been rather lonely around here without you," the brown-haired commandant said to the handsome, blue-eyed, flaxen-haired Aryan man.

"I missed you too."

"Did you get a haircut?" the commandant inquired.

"A Jew hairdresser gave me one in Beregszász."

"Brings out your pretty blue eyes. She made a good job."

"*He* made a good job. The barber was a man."

"A man? You were with someone else in Hungary, hey, Heimlich?"

"Of course not. He only gave me a haircut and a shave."

"Are you sure that's all the Jew-barber gave you?"

"Yes, Commandant. Are we finished with the interrogation?"

"I feel like you're not being entirely honest with me, Sergeant."

"Oh, please, spare me the melodrama."

"I was only joking. Lighten up, sweetheart."

The commandant picked up a heavy glass paperweight on the desk. He shook the object and watched as tiny snowflakes fell onto a miniature Christmas tree. A Santa Claus waved from inside the paperweight. It was a gift from his mother last year.

"Oh—I almost forgot," the sergeant said. "Mrs. Holstein gave me a telegram for you. The Headquarters of the High Command in Berlin sent it a few minutes ago. It's marked extremely important."

"Read it for me, Sergeant."

"Sent 9:00 a.m. June 2, 1944. Official business. To Commandant Graben. Mauthausen Concentration Camp· On July 4th, 1944, at exactly three o'clock in the afternoon, Major Wolfgang Himmel, Lieutenant Karl Flügel, and Captain Herman P. Segan will arrive in Mauthausen to make an official visit and inspection of the camp's facility. The officers' wives will accompany them. You will prepare accommodations and meals for the entourage of six guests, two soldiers, and one chauffeur. They will be staying at your private villa for two days and two nights.

Sincerely Yours,

Mrs. Helga T. Glockenspiel

Secretary to Führer Klaus von Hellmenz

Office of the SS High Command in Berlin"

"Let me see that," the commandant said.

The sergeant handed him the telegram.

"That's awfully odd," the commandant stated, noting the official seal of the SS High Command stamped on the top of the telegram. "I wonder why Berlin didn't give me more notice about this matter."

"I'm sure the *führer* has his reasons," the sergeant stated.

"Suppose you're right. You'll have to organize a proper welcoming party for the visitors. Inform the steward and the head chef immediately. We must have the finest food, champagne, and wine. Call your friend, Prior Mueller at the monastery. See if he can procure some of that Benedictine and Brandy, and cheese they make there. Get an extra case of wine also. No skimping. Understood, Heimlich?"

"*Ja,* of course."

"*Wunderbar.* Has the electric fence been repaired yet?" the commandant questioned.

"Prisoner Zugreb said it was done this morning. By the way, the electrician knows a couple of new prisoners who have valuable work skills."

"What kind of skills?"

"One's a shoemaker," the sergeant replied. "The other man is a glazier."

"Where are they working now?"

"At the quarry."

"Have the two prisoners in my office this afternoon," the commandant said. "And I want you go to town and have our dress uniforms cleaned and pressed. I suggest you take a bath first."

"Anything else while I'm in town?"

"Yes, sweetheart," the commandant replied. "Why don't you get us a few bottles of that dark beer I like. And two fat ham sandwiches on pumpernickel. Extra mustard on mine. And do me a huge favor while you're in town—get yourself a nice bottle of cologne. And get one for Corporal Wagner, also. Put everything on the Mauthausen account."

"*Ja.*"

"And one more thing," the commandant said while the sergeant looked back from the open doorway.

"*Ja?*"

"Don't forget the half-sour pickles."

12

In the late afternoon, a *Kübelwagen* transported Ben and Mr. Katz from the quarry back to the camp and directly to the commandant's office. The men's pajama-like uniforms were still covered with a fine white dust. While the commandant leisurely finished the other half of his ham sandwich and wiped some mustard off his brown mustache, he turned up his nose and inspected the yellow Jewish stars sewn onto the men's shirts. The color reminded him of the dandelion he had plucked that morning. He squashed his cigarette in an ashtray and addressed the two men.

"My name is Commandant Graben, and this is my faithful assistant, Sergeant Heimlich. I was informed that one of our trusted electricians recommended both of you." The commandant admired Ben's strong physique a moment. "What's your name, muscleman?"

"Benjamin Weiss."

"What type of work do you do, Weiss?"

"I'm a glazier."

"You can fix broken windows?"

"*Ja*, Commandant Graben."

"Do you know how to cut glass?"

"*Ja.*"

"Are you skilled at it?"

"I'm not a master glazier—almost a journeyman."

"That should do," the commandant said as he took a hand-brush and cleaned the dust from Ben's yellow Jewish star. He squeezed Ben's strong bicep muscle. "But if you don't do a good job, Weiss... you'll hang from the gallows. Is that clear?"

"I understand, Commandant."

"*Gut.* Tomorrow morning, I want you to install three mirrors inside the guest rooms at my private villa. A window at the officers' dining room needs to be repaired also. Go with the sergeant. He will show you where your tools are located."

"*Danke schön,* Commandant."

"*Bitte schön.*"

Ben and the sergeant left the office while Mr. Katz waited for his interrogation. He nervously cracked his knuckles and rubbed his calloused hands while watching the fish dart through the aquarium. The commandant stood at his desk and opened a gold-plated cigarette box. He removed two cigarettes.

"You like my fish?"

"I do. I used to have an aquarium back home."

"Where was your home?"

"In Beregszász, Hungary."

"Cigarette?"

"No, thank you. I don't smoke."

"What's your name, Jew?"

"Jacob Katz."

"The shoemaker, I presume?"

"*Ya*, Commandant. I'm sorry, my German isn't so good."

"I can speak Hungarian if you'd prefer. How long have you been a shoemaker?"

"Twenty-five years."

"I want you to make me a pair of black dress boots. With a zipper on the side. Can you do that?"

"If you provide me with the shoe leather and—"

The commandant interrupted, "Your tools and materials will be at your new workbench in the maintenance building. We'll go there shortly. I want the boots in six days. If not—you'll go back to work at the quarry. Do you understand, Katz?"

"*Igen*, Commandant."

"Now measure my feet," the commandant said, while he tossed Mr. Katz a cloth measuring tape. The officer sat down and placed his legs up onto his desk. "Take off my boots."

* * *

Ben and the sergeant walked through the garage yard and into the camp's maintenance building. Various tradesmen momentarily looked up from their workbenches as the two men went over to a square table covered with a thin rug. The sergeant pulled a chain that illuminated a single light bulb above the table. A yellowish-white light shone down.

"This is your work area, Prisoner Weiss. All your tools, glass, and mirror of various measurements are here. Can you think of anything else you might need for the job?"

"A glass cutter might come in handy," Ben replied.

"Yes, I have them right here," the sergeant said as he pulled a small cardboard box from his shirt pocket. It contained two brand-new diamond-blade glass cutters. "Don't lose them. They were expensive. You'll be responsible for keeping all the tools secure. If they get lost or stolen—you'll be punished. Here's the key for your tool locker. Lock it at the end of your shift. You'll work six days a week. Monday through Saturday. In exchange for the work, you'll receive camp money to purchase various goods at the prison commissary. The money can also be used to pay for the services of a young woman in the camp brothel. Unless you happen to be a homosexual that is. In which case you would have to make other arrangements."

The sergeant glanced at Ben with an unchaste grin.

"I'm not a homosexual," he stated.

"Regardless. This is your work pass. It will allow you to go unaccompanied anywhere in the camp. All you have to do is show it to the guards or kapos. *Gut?*"

"*Ja.*"

The sergeant gave Ben a small yellow document with his name hand-printed and the sergeant's signature below it.

"I want your work area cleaned and organized. After, you'll go to the administration building, and the commandant's secretary will validate your work pass. When you enter the building, go down the hall; her office is the first door on the left. It's imperative you address her as Mrs. Holstein. She's right next to the office you were in this afternoon. Meet me here tomorrow morning. Six-thirty sharp. Don't be late, or I'll dock you a whole day's pay. Do you have any questions, prisoner Weiss?"

"*Nein.*"

"Now work."

After Ben swept and organized his work area, he shut off the light over his worktable and headed for the administration building. Inside, he passed the portraits in the hall, and knocked on Mrs. Holstein's door.

Her stern voice loudly called from within. "Enter!"

Ben reluctantly opened the door and awkwardly stood with the yellow work pass in his hand.

"What do you want, Jew?" the secretary snapped.

"Sorry to disturb you, Mrs. Holstein. Sergeant Heimlich sent me here to have my work pass stamped."

The redhead glanced up as she folded a paper and stuffed it inside a white envelope. She spit on an Austrian postage stamp that displayed the führer's dog-bitten face.

"Come in, Jew. Close the door."

He shut it and slowly approached Mrs. Holstein's desk as she sprayed herself with a floral perfume. She lifted the hem on her skirt and displayed her pale upper thighs. She bent over and pulled open a bottom drawer. Searching through it, she freely exposed her cleavage to Ben. His eyes widened a bit.

"Where is that damn thing!" She looked up. "What are you staring at, Jew?"

"Nothing," Ben said, rapidly diverting his eyes to the wall.

"Don't lie! I can tell you were looking at me. You find me attractive?"

Ben thought for a moment.

"*Oh.*"

"Oh, what?" she asked.

"*Ja.* You are attractive, Mrs. Holstein."

"*Danke schön.* If you'd said anything less, I would have sent you to the gas chambers. Give me the work pass."

He handed her the yellow document.

"My validation stamper must be in the commandant's office. Follow me," she said, picking up the stamped envelope.

They walked to the office next door.

"Wait outside," she ordered.

The secretary cracked open the door without knocking. She quietly entered.

"Commandant, I finished your mother's letter, if you'd like to read it. And I need to validate a prisoner's work pass—have you seen the stamper?"

The secretary covered her mouth in surprise.

"I put it on your shelf," the commandant snapped in reply. "Now get out of here!"

Mrs. Holstein dropped the envelope, at the sight of the commandant's bare white ass. His pants had been pulled down to the top of his boots. A hand that wasn't his own, clutched him behind his hip.

"I said—get out!"

* * *

That evening, back in Barracks 20 at the supper table, Zohar squeezed between Ben and Mr. Katz; he set down his ration of hard bread and watery soup, then briefly bowed his head and prayed.

"Good evening, gentlemen," Zohar greeted. "Pass the salt, please."

"Good evening, Zohar," Ben said as he reached for a metal shaker with holes in the top; he handed it to the electrician. "We'd like to thank you for getting us our new work assignments."

"You're welcome. Are your workbenches in the maintenance building?"

"*Igen.*"

"Mine's there also," Zohar mentioned. "The commandant will be throwing a big party at his villa in a few days. I've worked his parties before. It's an easy job.

And he pays well. He'll need two extra men to help out in the kitchen and dining room. You'll have plenty of delicious food to eat. Either of you interested?"

"I'm in," Ben replied.

"Me too," Mr. Katz added.

"Good. I'll inform Sergeant Heimlich tomorrow morning. Pass the water, please."

13

Bells rang out through the halls of an elementary school in the village of Mauthausen, signaling the end of classes that day and the official start of summer vacation. A teacher, Mrs. Eichholtz, erased the history lesson on the chalkboard while three fifth-grade boys grabbed their book bags and lunch boxes and dashed out of the classroom before anyone else. Hans, Peter, and Adolf cut through a neatly landscaped school yard, went through a green gate, and then happily walked to the neighborhood where they lived.

"Now that summer vacation is here—we'll be able to enlist in the Nazi youth brigade," said the flaxen-haired boy named Adolf.

"*Ja*, Adolf, I'm really excited about it," Hans mentioned while his blue eyes widened. "A cousin of mine who lives in Frankfurt said his unit gets to shoot live ammunition sometimes."

"Oh, yeah. What do they shoot, Hans?" Peter inquired as the boys stopped to drink water from their army canteens.

"Jews—of course."

Adolf laughed as he bent down to tie his shoelaces. "And do you think your cousin is telling the truth, Hans?"

"I don't know. Why?"

"Just wondering," the flaxen-haired youth named Adolf answered, while four girls with long yellowish pigtails giggled past them.

"Shall we play by the camp today, boys?" Peter asked. "Maybe we'll see something exciting."

"*Ja.* We'll meet at my house this time," Adolf replied. "Don't forget to bring your binoculars, Hans."

* * *

Once the three schoolboys returned to their homes, they changed into play clothes, wolfed down milk and cookies, and then kissed their mothers goodbye. Hans and Peter ran to their friend's house and rang the doorbell.

"Hello, boys," Adolf's mother smilingly greeted from the open doorway.

"Hello, Mrs. Eichmann," the other two boys said.

The woman's golden-haired son grabbed his water canteen and came outside.

"See you later, *mutter,*" Adolf told his mother, and kissed her on the cheek before running off to play.

"Don't be late for supper, Adolf."

"*Nein, mutter,*" her son called back from the street.

A cat rubbed against Mrs. Eichmann's leg as she watered her multicolored pansies beside the porch.

* * *

Hans, Peter, and Adolf crossed over some railroad tracks by their neighborhood, and they headed into the woods, where they hiked a trail for a kilometer or so. A steep gravel road led them to the Mauthausen concentration camp. The youths climbed a tall oak tree planted on the other side of an electric barbed wire fence, their favorite spot. From the lofty perspective, they clearly observed hundreds of naked inmates inside the spacious garage yard.

"That's disgusting," Hans remarked, "The prisoners aren't wearing any clothes."

"The guards are spraying something on them," Adolf said.

"That's to get rid of their lice," Peter stated. "My father told me. He delivers milk to the camp twice a week."

"Does he?" Hans inquired.

"Ja."

In a more distant view, emaciated prisoners, almost ant-like in size, were climbing the staircase of death inside the Wiener Graben rock quarry. Hans peered through his binoculars and observed several prisoners who were standing at the very top of the quarry staircase. Guards stood behind them and pushed the prisoners off the cliff with the ends of their rifles. The men flew off and landed on the hard quarry floor, alive for only a few moments.

"Oh, my God ... that's terrible," Hans said, holding onto his tree branch and viewing the atrocity through his field glasses.

"Let me have a look, Hans," Adolf requested as he reached for his friend's binoculars.

"Here—be careful—it's not a pretty sight."

Peter braced himself against a thick oak limb, and he checked the time on his wristwatch. It was three o'clock on the dot. The youth curiously watched as a dull gray *Kübelwagen,* and a glossy blue Mercedes drove up to the camp's guard gate and stopped.

Peter pointed, "Look how shiny that car is, boys!"

The other two took notice.

"*Hei!*" Adolf exclaimed in German. "That is shiny. It must be a brand-new car."

"*Ja* ... it's splendid," Hans added.

The sentry at the guard gate raised his arm.

"*Heil Hellmenz,*" greeted the soldiers inside the *Kübelwagen.*

"*Heil Hellmenz*," Corporal Wagner said, squinting through his coke-bottle lenses. "What is the purpose of your visit to Mauthausen?"

"We're from the High Command in Berlin," replied one of the soldiers. "The high-ranking officers and their wives are behind us."

"Wait here while I get clearance from the commandant," the corporal said. He picked up a black phone and dialed the number for the commandant's villa.

"Graben speaking."

"It's Corporal Wagner, Commandant. The high-ranking officers have arrived from Berlin."

"*Wunderbar.* Tell them someone will come down to meet them in a few minutes."

"*Jawohl.*"

The poor-sighted corporal hung up the phone and addressed the soldier who was leading the entourage.

"You're clear to pass—park by the *Kübelwagen*—someone will meet you there shortly," the corporal informed the soldier.

"*Danke.*"

"*Bitte.* And welcome to Mauthausen."

The corporal raised the camp's front gate, and the ultra-blue Mercedes and the lackluster gray military vehicle drove through. They parked, and the driver of the blue Mercedes helped the officers' wives out of the limo while their husbands lingered inside a few minutes.

The three women chatted with each other, taking little interest in Mauthausen's vulgar granite facade. They wore identical mink stoles over red satin blouses, white gloves, pleated black skirts, stockings with garter belts, polished red heels, and pretentious black hats with hanging white tassels. One woman opened her umbrella and shielded herself from the bright sunlight. Another woman checked her heavily made-up face in a compact mirror, while the third woman casually smoked from a gold-plated cigarette holder. They watched as a guard relentlessly beat a prisoner chained to a stone wall nearby. The poor man displayed an inverted pink triangle on his bloodstained shirt, identifying him as a homosexual. The prisoner screamed for mercy, and the women turned their gazes away from the brutal spectacle. One of them spoke as she opened a silk hand-fan painted with Japanese flowers.

"Why must there be such a flagrant display of cruelty right here at the front entrance?"

"I don't know, Greta," replied the woman who looked at her face in the compact mirror. "It's rather barbaric if you want my opinion."

"I must agree. It certainly doesn't leave me with a good impression of the place."

"I have to pee soon," said the woman under the shade umbrella.

"Me too."

"Perhaps we should wait till we get somewhere more civilized," said the woman fanning herself. "I don't suggest we use the facilities inside the camp."

"I hope that won't be too long, girls, or I just might wet my undies," Greta, the major's wife, joked.

The women cackled while their husbands climbed out of the car and donned their military caps. The three officers focused on the tall oak tree on the other side of the electric fence. They waved to the boys who were perched high up in the tree. The youths held onto their branches and waved back. A pride welled up in them, seeing the officers' handsome military uniforms decorated with gold and silver medallions. The next moment, the boys watched as the three officers suddenly turned into angels. Each of them had a set of wings: one a bright crimson red; another a dazzling gold; and the third a lustrous blue, like the paint on the Mercedes. The youths felt a loving warmth wash over their bodies while the angels' faces glowed a fiery orange.

"Hans, Adolf! Do you see what I see?" Peter nervously inquired.

"Yes, we do," the other two boys replied in unison.

Hans accidentally dropped his binoculars, and they fell on the hard ground below. The youths were awestruck. The celestial beings instantly turned back into high-ranking officers. In a panic, the three boys hurriedly climbed down from the tall, majestic oak. Hans retrieved his binoculars before they left their fantastic playground behind. The boys ran until they reached the shaded trail, where they stopped to catch their breaths. They gazed into each other's excited eyes. Hans examined his field glasses.

"Are they broken?" Peter asked him.

"Strange . . . not even a scratch. We must have been dreaming before," Hans said.

"It was real, Hans," Peter said. "I saw it with my own eyes. We must promise ourselves never to tell a soul about what we saw back there. Not even our mothers or fathers."

"They wouldn't believe us anyway," Adolf stated.

"If we told anyone, we'd be locked up in the insane asylum," Peter said.

"I agree," Adolf added. "They would take us to Hartheim Castle. That's where the Nazis are poisoning Jews—and the mentally insane. We'll promise to keep this to ourselves."

"*Ja.*"

Peter glanced at the time on his wristwatch. "Let's go—we'll be late for supper."

Hans, Peter, and Adolf were greatly changed after what they had experienced that day. And they vowed never to join the Nazi Youth Movement, nor enlist in the military, nor go anywhere near the concentration camp ever again.

Back at the camp, the high-ranking officers turned from the tree and observed the hilly landscape in the opposite direction.

"There's nothing like the sweet innocence of youth," Major Himmel mentioned to his colleagues.

"I agree, Major," Captain Segan said as he picked a glowing red feather off his sleeve.

The major looked through his binoculars and saw an old terracotta building with two wooden crosses on the roof. He lowered the field glasses and pointed his finger. "That might be a monastery over there," he mentioned. "I heard there was one close by."

"Let me have a look?" the lieutenant asked his superior officer.

Sergeant Heimlich kicked up a small white cloud of gravel as he marched over to greet the three dignitaries and their wives. The sergeant was startled by the radiant blue car in the background.

"*Heil Hellmenz*, officers, ladies. My name is Sergeant Heimlich. Welcome to Mauthausen."

"*Heil Hellmenz*, Sergeant," the major greeted.

The officers saluted back; their wives politely smiled and wrinkled their noses, because of the sergeant's freshly applied cologne. He had put on more than was necessary.

"Sergeant, I'm Major Wolfgang Himmel, and this is my wife, Greta. Lieutenant Karl Flügel, his lovely wife, Hannah. And this is Captain Herman P. Segan, and his dear wife, Maria."

"I'm extremely pleased to meet you all," the sergeant said.

"We've heard a lot about you back in Berlin," the major mentioned, releasing his firm grip on the sergeant's hand.

"You have?" the sergeant asked in a confused tone. He felt a strange energy circulate inside his chest.

"Of course," the major replied. "We know more than you would believe, Sergeant."

"Everyone will be staying at the guest quarters in the commandant's private villa," the sergeant announced. "Cocktails and hors d'oeuvres are scheduled two hours from now. We'll have a lovely dinner afterwards."

"*Wunderbar,* Sergeant. Where is the commandant's villa located?" the major inquired.

"Not far from here. Have your soldiers and chauffeur follow me."

"I don't mind riding with you."

"You're most welcome, Major . . . but I'm certain my *Kübelwagen* isn't as comfortable as your Mercedes."

"I like to rough it sometimes," the major said, turning toward the sergeant's army vehicle.

The three women and the other two officers got back inside the blue limo, and the driver and their military escort followed the sergeant's *Kübelwagen* out of the camp, then onto a well-paved road for about a kilometer. The three vehicles climbed a steep hill and up a long driveway; at the top, a secluded villa appeared.

From a bedroom window on the second floor of the villa, Commandant Graben espied the glowing blue Mercedes. He snorted another line of cocaine while his butler turned a gold-plated faucet in the bathroom, filling a brass-footed tub with hot water and liquid to make a lavender-scented bubble bath.

The sergeant parked the *Kübelwagen,* and he quickly opened the door for the major.

"This is it," he announced.

"Gorgeous property," the major remarked, seeing a curtain conceal a face behind the bedroom window.

The three officers and their wives inhaled a pleasant evergreen fragrance from a nearby pine forest. Everyone was treated to an amazing view of the River Danube far below.

"It's beautiful up here," the major's wife mentioned. She admired some scarlet begonias bordering a white flagstone walkway. Bougainvillea plants hung along a wrap-around porch.

"Peaceful, isn't it," Lieutenant Flügel's wife remarked to her husband.

"*Ja . . .* extremely."

The sergeant escorted everyone to a side entrance of the villa. The two foot-soldiers followed the entourage from behind, carrying in the guests' luggage and their garment bags.

"These are the guest rooms you'll be staying in," the sergeant announced. "Each one has a private bathroom. Major, you and your wife will have the largest room at the end of the hall. There's a heated whirlpool tub on the deck outside. You'll find it most relaxing for tired muscles."

"*Wunderbar,*" the major said while his wife and the other two women quickly proceeded to the largest guest room down the hall.

"This is your room, Lieutenant," the sergeant announced.

"Such a beautiful marble tile," he remarked about the sleek white floor.

"That's not marble, Lieutenant," the sergeant stated. "It's polished granite."

"And why so much of it?"

The sergeant smirked and nonchalantly replied, "The cheap cost of labor and materials."

"The commandant must have a good friend in the construction business," Major Himmel said.

"The camp prisoners built the villa, Major," the sergeant stated. "The stone for the walkways, floors, kitchen counters, and bathroom vanities all came from the granite quarry near the camp. It didn't cost us one *pfennig.* Well . . . the workers received a minimal wage of course. Those who were fortunate enough to survive the construction project."

"I see," Major Himmel said.

"Our butler will come for you in two hours," the sergeant informed the officers. "Make yourselves at home. I'll show your soldiers and driver where their sleeping quarters will be."

"*Wunderbar.*"

Meanwhile, in the most spacious guest room down the hall, the officers' wives made light conversation with each other. Hannah Flügel glanced at a portrait of Führer Hellmenz above a large brass bed. "There he is again," she said while lifting her feathery brown eyebrows.

"Yes, I see his face everywhere now, it seems," Greta Himmel remarked as she kicked off her red high heels.

"Seriously," Mrs. Flügel critiqued, "He's not a very attractive looking man, is he?"

"*Nein*," Mrs. Segan said. "He ought to do something about that pathetic-looking mustache for heaven's sake. It looks like he stuck some horse manure under his nose."

The women exploded into a boisterous laughter. Moments later their husbands walked into the room, interrupting their jovial atmosphere.

"Sorry I missed the punch line, Greta," the major said. "What's so funny?"

"We were just having a little girl talk."

"Come, Hannah, we'll nap before we meet the commandant," the lieutenant said, nudging his wife's arm.

"You as well, Maria," the captain said to his spouse.

The two couples left the guest room, and Greta finally got to go to the bathroom. The major stood in front of a window that looked out onto a redwood deck, where the whirlpool tub sat. *We'll have to take a soak tonight,* he thought, as he closed the drapes. He unbuttoned his white shirt, unbuckled his belt, unzipped his pants, and then tiredly plopped onto an armchair where he pulled off his well-worn yet polished Nazi boots. He combed a hand through his thick growth of silvery-blue chest hair, noticing the portrait of Führer Hellmenz over the bed. The major pulled up his nose, knitted his brow, and touched a silver crucifix. He made the sign of the cross.

"Greta?"

"Yes, darling?" she answered from the bathroom.

"Will you be having a bath before we meet the commandant?"

"I will. Why?" she asked, brushing her voluminous blond hair in the bathroom mirror.

The major remained silent.

His wife came out dressed only in her blue stockings and white silk panties. She stood smiling in front of her husband, with the most broad and brilliant blue wings an angel could ever have.

"What were you saying, darling?" Greta Himmel asked.

14

Crystal chandeliers and shimmering candlelight illuminated the living room at the villa. The three high-ranking officers and their wives made their grand entrance to the gala hosted by Commandant Graben and Sergeant Heimlich. The three women wore elegant silk evening gowns, blue, gold, and red. Sparkling jewels beautified their necks, earlobes, fingers, and wrists. Their husbands were handsomely attired in jet-black formal military uniforms and high dress boots. Welcoming the guests, a classical pianist in a tux, one wild, gray-haired, long-nosed prisoner from the camp, sat next to a baby grand piano and deftly performed a nocturne composed by Chopin.

Zohar Zugreb loomed behind the bar in the living room. Happily smiling at the guests, the lanky Hungarian from Budapest was decked in a pair of tuxedo pants, starched white shirt, silk bow tie, and shiny black shoes; he was the official barman for the evening. The wild-haired piano player was startled when Zohar popped the cork from a bottle of ultra-expensive champagne; the pianist played three wrong notes but quickly regained his finesse, running his hands up and down the ivory keys. The commandant turned a critical eye toward the musician while Zohar poured the bubbly into eight glasses that sat on a walnut credenza.

Everyone picked up their champagne glasses, and the commandant toasted: "Here's to our most welcome guests."

"Cheers."

"*Prost.*"

"*Prost.*"

"You have a gorgeous home, Commandant," the major commented, admiring an ornately framed oil painting on a wall near the piano.

"Thank you, Major. That's an original Rembrandt, by the way. It's his *Holy Family with Angels.*"

"I'm quite familiar with the painting," the major stated. "Tell me . . . how did you acquire such a rare and valuable piece of artwork?"

"It once belonged to a wealthy Jewish family who lived in Vienna."

"Serious art lovers, I gather?" the major asked.

"*Ja.* The owner was the curator of the Wien art museum in Vienna. On the Karlsplatz."

"I know where it is, Commandant."

The major moved closer to the painting and saw that Rembrandt's signature had been scrawled on the bottom of the canvas.

"It's definitely authentic," he said. "It must have cost you a pretty penny—if you don't mind me asking—what was the price?"

The commandant grinned through his tightly clenched teeth. Before he answered, the commandant lit a smoke, sipped some more champagne, and brushed a glittering piece of lint off his handsome dress uniform; he briefly noticed the unusual thread as it fell to the polished granite floor.

"I didn't buy the painting, Major. We just removed it from the Jew's home."

"Oh?"

"The family had no use for it anymore," the commandant dryly stated. "Not where they were going."

"I see."

"The commandant has the loveliest furniture, Sergeant," Mrs. Himmel said, as the group migrated toward the lounge for appetizers and cocktails.

"*Danke schön,* Mrs. Himmel. *We* spent five tedious weeks decorating the house. The lounge is this way, ladies."

Mrs. Flügel whispered into Mrs. Segan's ear, "What do you suppose he meant by we? You don't think he and the commandant—are together—do you?"

"It's possible," Mrs. Segan replied as she raised her wrist and flaunted her diamond-studded bracelet. "Come on, I'm thirsty. I need a good stiff drink already."

Decked in their shiny black shoes, tuxedo pants, shirts, and silk bow ties, Ben and Mr. Katz readied themselves with trays in the lounge, preparing to serve the honored guests hot and cold delicacies: Swedish meatballs, pigs in a blanket, chicken liver in puff pastry, caviar, smoked salmon canapes, and deviled eggs.

Ben rubbed the birthmark on the side of his nose.

"What would the lovely ladies like to drink?" the sergeant inquired, helping himself to a caviar on toast.

"A dry martini for me, please," the major's wife replied.

"I'll have a Bloody Mary. *Bitte,*" Mrs. Flügel said.

"A scotch on the rocks," Mrs. Segan ordered.

"Make their drinks, Zugreb."

"Igen, Sergeant."

After Zohar made the women's cocktails, he served the lieutenant a gin and tonic, the captain a rum and coke.

Major Himmel walked up to the bar and inquired, "Do you happen to have some of that American whiskey? You know, the one that's made in Tennessee."

Zohar reached for a bottle on the top shelf. He smiled and asked, "You mean Jack Daniels?"

"Yes, yes . . . with a couple of ice-cubes, *bitte.*"

"Perhaps you would like a double, Major?"

"*Ja,* that would be excellent."

"Have you heard about the new mobile gassing units yet, Major?" Commandant Graben inquired.

Zohar served the major his drink.

"*Danke.* I haven't, but I'm definitely interested in knowing more about them," the major replied. "Do they run on diesel or standard gasoline?"

"I believe diesel. But I could be wrong," the commandant answered. "Dachau recently acquired two of the units. They're finding them highly efficient. The gas chambers in the trucks are hermetically sealed and can fit maybe seventy prisoners inside. Once the poison gas is pumped in, the occupants are dead within ten or fifteen minutes."

"Saves bullets," Sergeant Heimlich added with a smirk. "Would you like one of my American cigarettes, Major?"

"*Nein.* I don't smoke."

Ben came around with a tray of pigs in a blanket.

"I'll take one of those, Jew," Commandant Graben said.

Wearing his clean white gloves, Ben presented the finger food on a napkin, and the commandant dipped it in mustard. Ben cordially offered one to the major.

"No, thank you. I'm a vegetarian."

"Our gas chamber has been running nonstop since we closed the one at Hartheim castle," the sergeant stated. "How long would it take to requisition a couple of those mobile units, Major?"

"I'm not sure. I'll look into it when we return to Berlin." The tall high-ranking officer stood and lifted his glass, "I would like to propose a toast."

Glowing elegantly in their evening wear, the officers' wives lifted their glasses along with everyone else. Ben balanced his tray of appetizers and listened while Major Himmel spoke:

"To everyone's health. And a most enjoyable stay in Mauthausen."

"*Prost*, Major," the commandant said.

"*Prost.*"

"*Prost.*"

Sergeant Heimlich raised his cosmopolitan, and he also made a toast. "To the success of the *final solution*.

May the Third Reich never rest until every Jew is wiped off the face of the planet."

"*Prost*, everyone," the commandant added.

"*Prost.*"

"God forbid," Ben coughed under his breath.

The sergeant looked suspiciously at Ben; he inquired, "Did you say something, muscleman?"

"A pig under a blanket, sir?"

"*Nein*," the sergeant replied, as he rubbed his nose and mumbled *pigdog* in German, "*Schweinehund.*"

Major Himmel plopped on a bar stool, and he glanced down and admired the commandant's spiffy new boots. "Where did you get those from?" he asked.

The commandant threw back a scotch on the rocks, then signaled for Zohar to make him another.

"What are you referring to, Major?"

"Your boots. Love the style."

"Our shoemaker at the camp made them—how do they look on me?"

"Classy. He does excellent work," the major replied. "And ... are they comfortable? Sometimes new boots tend to be a little stiff until you break them in."

The commandant cleared his throat. "Pardon the cliché, Major. They fit like a glove."

"Could you arrange for your shoemaker to make *me* a pair?"

"Absolutely, Major. The shoemaker is standing right next to your wife. I'll call him over. You can speak to him yourself. Prisoner Katz, come here, please."

Mr. Katz had a hearing disability in one ear, and he didn't readily respond. Plus, the saxophone jazz of Charlie Parker blared on a Victrola, making it even more difficult for him to hear.

"Katz! Heimlich, do me a big favor?"

"*Ja*, Commandant?"

"Bring me that belligerent Jew—the shoemaker."

"*Jawohl.*"

Sergeant Heimlich approached Mr. Katz from behind and startled him by firmly rapping on his shoulder. The server dropped a whole tray of caviar canapes onto the floor; some of the fish eggs spilled onto the bottom of Mrs. Flügel's glowing red evening gown.

"*Schweinehund!*" the sergeant shouted. "Now look what you've done. Clean up this mess, Jew."

Mr. Katz quickly got on his hands and knees and picked up the food and nervously placed it onto the serving tray. Ben dampened a napkin and offered to wipe Mrs. Flügel's dress. She granted him permission.

The commandant walked over and asked, "What's going on here?"

"This *dummkopf* dropped a whole tray of expensive caviar," the sergeant replied. "Look... he stained the woman's dress."

"Don't be so hard on the man," Mrs. Flügel said. "It was only an accident."

The commandant whispered into the sergeant's ear, "Have the guards take him to the execution room immediately. And while you're at it—the piano player can go with him."

"*Jawohl.* Prisoner Weiss, finish cleaning this mess," the sergeant said.

"I apologize for the inconvenience, Mrs. Flügel," the commandant said. "I'll have someone bring you more caviar right away."

"That won't be necessary—I've lost my appetite for your stinky fish eggs," she said, then brusquely turned to the other women.

"Get up, Jew," the sergeant said, as he pulled Mr. Katz off the floor. "Come with me."

The sergeant went into the living room and approached the wild-haired man who sat at the piano. He yanked him from the bench and took him and Mr.

Katz outside to the wrap-around porch. The sergeant approached two guards who were smoking cigarettes.

"Bring these two prisoners back to the camp and have them liquidated."

"*Jawohl*, Sergeant. With pleasure."

* * *

A guard brought the piano player and Mr. Katz into a building and down a flight of stairs. He put them inside a dismal room where five other prisoners sat. One of the prisoners noticed the formally dressed men: "You two look like you just came from a wedding."

"What is this place?" Mr. Katz asked the other prisoner.

"The kapo said we were brought here to be photographed."

"Why?" the piano player inquired.

"I don't know. Better you not ask too many questions."

A kapo came into the room and tugged on the shirt of the man sitting next to Mr. Katz. The kapo brought the man into a smaller room and seated him on a chair that sat flush against a wall. Above the chair, a round hole had been cut into the wall. A gun barrel was placed through the opening, and it pointed toward the back of the prisoner's head. The kapo ordered the prisoner, "Look at the camera and smile." The kapo left the cubicle. On the reverse side of the wall, someone pulled a trigger, killing the prisoner who was seated on the chair. The executioner went outside for a cigarette and fresh air while two prisoners removed the dead man from the cubicle and another prisoner came in with a bucket of water and quickly cleaned the bloody brains off the wall. After several minutes, the next victim was brought inside the execution room, and he was seated against the wall.

* * *

Back at the villa, the chef and his helpers made the final preparations for dinner while the commandant and the sergeant joked with the three high-ranking officers at the bar. Their wives sat at a table and socialized among themselves.

"*Ja*... that's pretty funny, Major," the commandant stated. "Another whiskey, Zohar."

"Did you hear the one about the—" the sergeant began, until Major Himmel interrupted him.

"What happened to the waiter that was here earlier, Sergeant?" the major asked.

"Which one?"

"The shoemaker. I wanted to speak to him about making me a new pair of boots."

"He was taken to the execution room back at the camp," the sergeant stated.

"Are you out of your fucking minds?" the major shouted.

The three women looked uneasily toward the bar.

"He's probably dead by now," the sergeant nonchalantly stated, before downing a shot of vodka.

"What?" the major shouted again. "How will I get my boots made if you kill the shoemaker? Take me to this execution room immediately."

"But Major—we'll be having dinner soon," the commandant said.

"That's an order!"

"Take him there now, Sergeant," the commandant said. "And use my car—it'll be faster."

* * *

A kapo escorted Mr. Katz inside the execution cubicle. He sat and smoothed his white tuxedo shirt.

"Sit up straight and look at the camera," the kapo said.

The sergeant drove the black Mercedes through the camp's guard gate and quickly parked. He and the major hurried into the cold gray building. The odor of blood lingered in the air. On the other side of the execution cubicle, a trigger was pulled, but the chamber jammed. The executioner took out his revolver and was about to stick it through the hole when the major and the sergeant walked up behind him.

"Don't shoot!" the major exclaimed, "There's been a mistake. Release the prisoner."

The man turned around and saw the major and the sergeant clothed in their military dress uniforms.

"I said release the prisoner—and bring him here," the major ordered once more.

"*Jawohl.* Kapo!"

A prisoner came running.

"*Ja?*"

"Take the man out and bring him here."

"*Jawohl.*"

The kapo helped Mr. Katz off the chair and led him out by his arm. Mr. Katz questioned the major and the sergeant with a confused look.

"You're going back to work," the sergeant told the shoemaker.

"What about the piano player? He's in there too," Katz mentioned.

"Go get him, Sergeant," the major ordered.

The sergeant went into the waiting room and brought out the wild-haired piano player. They took both prisoners outside and walked them to the car.

"Tuck in your shirts and straighten your bow ties," the major ordered.

"We need to piss bad," the prisoners said, before they got in the car.

"Do it here. Quickly."

* * *

On the drive back to the villa, Major Himmel turned around to the backseat and spoke to Mr. Katz in Hungarian.

"I want you to make me a pair of dress boots like you made the commandant."

"*Igen,*" the shoemaker affirmed in Hungarian. "I will have to measure your feet, though."

"Of course. I'll meet you at your workbench tomorrow afternoon at five o'clock."

15

At a table in the officers dining room of Mauthausen, the high-ranking officers and their wives enjoyed a late continental breakfast. Major Himmel swallowed a bite of apricot strudel before chasing it with a double espresso and water. He turned to Lieutenant Flügel.

"I've decided to let you and Captain Segan handle the briefing scheduled with the commandant this afternoon. It's such a beautiful day out, Greta and I will go for a relaxing ride through the countryside.

"*Jawohl*, Major."

"We should return sometime in the afternoon. You have any questions, Lieutenant?"

"*Nein*, Major. Don't worry. We will see to everything. You and Greta have yourselves a delightful day."

"*Danke schön.*"

* * *

Raphael drove the major's Mercedes along a country road, which eventually led them through a charming village called Melk. Buildings with granite facades and wooden houses painted pink, white, brown, and yellow lined a busy shopping street. They slowly passed a grocery store and bakery; a post office; a French restaurant; a dry cleaner; and a barber shop. Some of the local inhabitants and shop owners stopped to observe the brightly painted automobile as it drove by. Beyond the village, the car climbed a steep hill; at the top, a wooden sign pointed the direction toward Saint Clemens Benedictine Monastery. Two large crosses were mounted high atop the terracotta roof of a massive building. Raphael parked, got out, and then helped Major Himmel and his wife from the car.

"You can relax, Raphael. We'll return in less than two hours."

"*Gut*, Major."

* * *

Major Himmel and his wife meandered past statues of saints posted at the front square of the sprawling cloister. A fountain of stone cherubs spit streams of water in the air. On the north side of the monastery, the River Danube splashed up along the abbey's broad foundation. The Austrian Alps loomed farther to the south; in the east, ominous plumes of smoke hovered above Gusen; one of Mauthausen's sub-camps. The couple strolled arm-in-arm onto the grounds of Saint Clemens, while the sun gradually approached its zenith.

Laboring in a vegetable garden nearby, four black-robed monks wielded a rake, shovel, spade, and water hose. They warily observed the unexpected visitors. The major and his wife sat on a bench underneath the shade of a leafy English oak. They heard a distant rumbling, then watched as four B-17 bombers appeared over the horizon. The noisy aircraft boldly advanced like a rolling thunder; the monstrous air fleet passed overhead and left trails of thick, cottony exhaust. The major touched a strand of his wife's braided golden hair, and he breathed a deep sigh of relief. He contemplated the rich blueness of the sky.

"I'm really homesick, Greta."

"Me too, darling. Shall we go inside now?"

"*Ja.*"

The major and his wife left the bench under the leafy oak, and they walked by a clock tower proximal to the front entrance. A young monk tolled the bell for high noon as the major knocked on the pink front door of the monastery. Moments later, a hooded monk appeared.

"*Heil Hellmenz.* Can I help you, officer?"

"Good morning, brother. Or should I say, good afternoon. My name is Major Wolfgang Himmel. And this is my wife, Greta."

"Pleased to meet you, Mr. and Mrs. Himmel. I'm Prior Mueller. What can I do for you, Major?"

The strong afternoon sunlight blurred the prior's vision some. He put up his hand to block the glare.

"Prior . . . I'm here on official business from Berlin, and we were just taking a leisurely ride through the countryside when we saw the monastery. We thought it would make an interesting place to visit; my wife and I are devout Catholics."

"That's a good thing, Major. But if the abbot isn't expecting you, I'm afraid we can't allow any visitors today."

"Not even a quick tour?"

"We only give tours on Mondays, Tuesdays, and Saturdays," the prior said, growing more impatient.

"Are you sure you can't make an exception for us?" Mrs. Himmel pleaded. She charmingly smiled at the blond-bearded prior.

The prior frowned slightly, contemplating the major's authoritative red, black, and white swastika armband.

"I don't make the rules at the monastery, Major. I'll have to check with the abbot first."

"We understand."

"Come inside, then."

In the vestibule, the noon light streamed through a window below an arched ceiling, illuminating the visitors' burnished faces. Mesmerized by their glowing countenances, Prior Mueller stepped back a moment and observed a circle of bright white light around the major and his wife.

"Is there something wrong, Prior?" the major asked.

"No. I just noticed that you both have very healthy-looking skin. Wait here while I look for the abbot."

"*Danke schön.*"

* * *

Abbot Zebedee was not inside his office, so the prior closed his door and continued through the hallway until he came to a long spiral staircase. He held onto a wrought-iron handrail and cautiously ascended the tedious metal stairs. Painted on the ceiling high above the stairwell, frescoes exploded with vivid colors and seraphic themes. It was a long way up and a long way down. After climbing numerous steps, the prior eventually reached the top floor, where a voluminous library was housed. He entered a room filled with tall bookshelves, murals, and windows which offered panoramic views of the village, River Danube, and the Austrian Alps. He passed the unoccupied librarian's desk, walked through the inner sanctum of the book room, and then approached a scholarly man of great stature who was sitting at a table and studying an ancient Latin manuscript.

"I had a good feeling you might be up here," the prior greeted the abbot. "I'm sorry if I disturbed you."

"What is it now, Mueller?"

The broad Italian abbot uncovered his hood and removed his reading glasses, pensively rolling his eyes up at his blond-bearded assistant.

"A Nazi officer and his wife are waiting for you downstairs in the vestibule."

"What on earth for?" the abbot inquired.

"He asked if they could meet with you. Perhaps get a look around the abbey."

"Why didn't you tell him I was busy?"

"I tried ... but they were persistent. Said they were devout Catholics."

"Tell him to get lost," the abbot said. "You know we don't give tours on Wednesdays. And since when have Nazis ever been devout Catholics? Seems a bit ironic, don't you think?"

The abbot turned a page in the manuscript, put on his reading glasses again, and focused on the Latin text.

"He came from Berlin, Abbot. He said he was a high-ranking officer."

"Big deal. What am I supposed to do with these God-damn Nazis already? Royal pains in my ass. *Forgive me, Lord.* Go downstairs and accompany them to my office. Heat up some water in the tea kettle. And tell the *Capitan* and his wife I'll be there shortly."

The prior corrected the abbot before leaving, "I believe he said he was a major."

"What's the difference? They're all just rotten scumbags to me," he said under his breath. "Murderous lot. Forgive me, Lord."

The abbot closed the manuscript and slowly raised his large body. He plodded toward the librarian's desk, where Brother Martin was reading about Abraham and his wife, Sarah. He raised his eyes to the abbot.

"It's utterly amazing how Abraham's wife was able to conceive a child at ninety years old," the librarian stated. "It's downright miraculous."

"Yes, it is, Brother Martin. Miraculous. Have a blessed afternoon."

"You as well, Abbot. And be careful going down the stairs."

"Always."

The abbot lifted his robe with one hand and securely held the handrail with the other. He descended the spiral staircase, admiring the angelic murals along the way. At the bottom step, he paused to catch his breath and wipe his brow. The hem of his robe swished back and forth as he moved through the hallway. He opened the door to his office and saw the Nazi officer and his wife seated there.

"Greetings. And welcome to Saint Clemens Monastery. I'm Abbot Zebedee."

The major stood and politely shook the abbot's broad hand.

"It's a pleasure to make your acquaintance, Abbot. My name is Major Himmel. And this is my wife, Greta."

She smiled, removed her sun hat, stood, and offered the abbot her soft hand. The abbot held it gently and felt a warmth of energy a few moments. He saw that the woman's eyes gave off a peculiar blue scintillation.

The tea kettle whistled.

"Sit," the abbot said, motioning to the chairs. "Will you and your wife be joining me for a cup of tea?"

"That's most gracious of you," the major replied.

"Prior, would you prepare three teas, please."

"Yes, Abbot."

"And what can I do for you, Major? I understand that you and your wife are interested in a tour of the monastery?"

"That won't be necessary, Abbot. Perhaps at a more convenient time. The main reason I'm here concerns the war effort."

"And how's that going?" the clergyman asked.

"War is a filthy business. I'd much rather see peace in Europe. I'll never understand why humans kill each other. When you come right down to it . . . we're all just brothers and sisters on this good earth."

"I definitely agree with you there," the abbot said, maneuvering his large body around to sit on a chair at his desk.

The prior asked, "Would our guests like sugar or honey in their tea? We make the honey at the monastery. Well . . . the bees do most of the work."

"A teaspoon of honey in both cups, please," the major replied.

"*Ja*, Major," the prior said, as he opened a jar of clover honey, added the sweetener, and then handed the major and his wife the teacups.

"*Danke schön.*"

"*Bitte schön.*"

"I've come here with a specific purpose in mind," Major Himmel announced.

"And what might that be?" the abbot asked.

"You must be familiar with Mauthausen."

"I grew up in the village," the abbot said. "I know the place like the back of my hand. My parents moved there from Rome when I was twelve."

"I meant the concentration camp," the major stated.

"Unfortunately, I am familiar with the camp," the abbot stated. "Sometimes the wind blows wrong and smoke from the crematorium seeps into the monastery. It's a most unpleasant experience."

"I'm sure of that," the major's wife sullenly chimed.

The abbot asked the prior to give him and his guests some privacy. "Prior, I need you go into town and buy some milk, please. Take the car keys."

"Yes, of course, Abbot. A pleasure meeting you and your wife, Major."

"Likewise."

Prior Mueller left the office and slowly closed the door. He stood in the hallway a few moments, hoping to catch some of the conversation inside. He put his ear toward the door. Sister Hildegard saw him as she strolled through the hallway. The nun gave the eavesdropping prior a disdainful glance.

"Shame on you, Prior—you know better than that."

He embarrassingly put his head down and quickly walked away.

Inside the office, the abbot grew more fidgety with his two guests.

Major Himmel patiently set his cup down, noticing a painting of the Vatican. He smiled at his wife.

"I'm going to bring you three Hungarian prisoners from the Mauthausen camp," the major announced.

"What for?"

"The commandant and I have decided they should work here."

"That's sort of odd," the abbot stated. "What kind of work do they do?"

"One's a shoemaker, one's an electrician, and one's a glazier. They're decent and hardworking men. And I'm sure there's plenty of work for them at the monastery."

"There is. But I don't know if it's such a good idea for Jews to come here and work."

"Why not?" the major asked, "They can live at the monastery as well. It would be more convenient for them."

The abbot scratched his large head and stirred his tea. He took a sip.

"I'd have to think it over first."

"Unfortunately, you don't have that option, Abbot. I already made arrangements with the commandant at Mauthausen."

The abbot looked up, befuddled.

"This is all so sudden, Major."

"Don't worry—it's for a good cause."

"The war effort?"

"So, to speak."

"How long will the men be at the monastery?" the abbot inquired.

"That all depends on how long the war lasts."

"When will they be coming?" the abbot asked.

"Tomorrow morning before sunrise. You'll receive them yourself. And provide them with three private rooms, meals, and clothing like the other monks wear. You'll treat them as if they were monks. And nobody at the monastery can know they came from Mauthausen. All except for Sister Hildegard. She can be trusted to tell. But definitely not Prior Mueller. If anyone asks you about the three new monks, tell them they were formerly at the Archabbey of Pannonhalma, in Hungary. Like I said before, the three men are Hungarians. Do you understand me, Abbot?"

"I do."

"Good. I'll need from you three monk's robes and three pairs of shoes," the major said. "Write all these sizes down."

The abbot took up a pencil and found some note paper.

"One man is tall. He should fit into a large robe. The other two robes would be a medium and a small. Their shoe sizes are seven, eight, and ten. Put the large size shoes with the large robe, the eight with the medium, and the seven with the small robe. They'll need new undergarments and socks as well. All the clothes and shoes should be placed in separate garment bags if you have them. I'll need it all now. After the clothes have been organized, my driver will help bring it out to the car."

The abbot picked up his phone. "I'll call the laundry and have someone prepare the clothes."

"Excellent," the major said while he reached into his pants pocket and took out a brown envelope and set it in front of the abbot.

After the abbot spent a few minutes on the phone, he hung up the receiver and asked the major about the envelope. "What's that?"

"Open it."

He tore open the envelope and found a thick wad of money in large denominations.

"It's ten thousand deutsche marks," the major stated. "A little donation for the monastery."

"Oh, that's most generous of you, Major! Thank you very much. I have gifts for you also," the abbot said, as he reached for a bottle on the shelf behind him. He smiled and set the bottle in front of the major. "It's from my private stock. And take this, Mrs. Himmel," he said, giving her a small bible inscribed with gold words. *Saint Clemens Monastery.*

"Thank you, Abbot," she told him.

"You're welcome."

"Ah! *Wunderbar*. Benedictine and brandy," the major said.

"And this is a gift for you also," the abbot said, handing the major's wife a bottle filled with golden clover honey. "It's made here, like the prior said."

"Oh, *danke schön*."

"Bitte schön."

"If it's possible, Abbot, my wife and I would like to pray in your chapel before we leave. We're both devout Catholics."

"Yes, of course. The prior informed me. Come, I'll show you where it is."

The major grabbed the Benedictine and brandy while his wife placed the bible and the jar of honey into her handbag.

Five o'clock that afternoon

In the camp's maintenance building, Ben cut a pane of glass and gently set it into a window frame; he smoothed a ribbon of putty along the edges and placed the repaired window aside. He lifted another window frame onto the worktable and proceeded to remove the hardened putty with a hammer and chisel. A welder looked up, scattering white sparks in the air. Major Himmel had entered the building, and most everyone stood at attention. Two carpenters paused from hammering three-penny nails into a truss, while the shrill sound of a circular saw came to a stop. Zohar, the electrician, was tinkering with the commandant's short-wave radio. He had tuned in a station from Berlin; the mad führer was screaming behind a static through the speaker. The radio was silenced while Mr. Katz stopped hammering a sole onto a boot when the major walked over to the cobbler's workbench.

"Good afternoon, Prisoner Katz. How are you doing today?"

Mr. Katz got off his stool. "Good afternoon, Major. I'm doing fine—thanks to you. Have a seat and I'll take those measurements."

The major smiled, took off his cap and sat on a chair. Mr. Katz raised one of the major's legs onto a short stool and removed his old boot. He took the other one off and proceeded to measure the length and width of the officer's feet. He wrote the dimensions on a piece of scrap paper.

"Do you want the boots with a zipper on the side?" the shoemaker asked.

"That'll be fine."

"Black or brown leather?"

"I prefer brown."

Mr. Katz added that info onto the scrap paper, then helped the major put on his boots.

"You're all set then," Mr. Katz said. They'll be ready for you next week. Do you want them mailed to Berlin?"

"I'm not in a rush, Mr. Katz. I'll get them when I see you at the monastery."

The shoemaker looked up puzzled. "I don't understand— Major—what do you mean by monastery?"

"I'll explain. Call the electrician and the glass-man over here."

"Ben! Zohar! Come here," Mr. Katz shouted above the noise inside the building. He waved them over. The two men stopped working, and they met at the cobbler's workbench.

"First off, I want to compliment everyone on the tremendous job you did on the party last night," the major said. "Each of you grab a milk crate and sit."

Ben and Zohar found milk crates and placed them by the shoemaker's workbench.

The major spoke in a fluent Hungarian: "The commandant and I have decided to give the three of you new work assignments. You'll be going to work at a monastery a few kilometers from here. It's called Saint Clemens. We've arranged for you to live there as well. Don't tell anyone in the camp you're leaving. Guards or otherwise. That's very important. From this moment on, you'll call yourselves Brother Jacob, Brother Benjamin, and Brother Zohar."

"What kind of work is it, Major?" Zohar asked.

"The same work you're doing here."

"What about tools?" Ben asked. "We have none of our own."

"You'll take the tools from here, but only what fits into a milk crate. Everything else you'll need; the monastery will provide. While you're at the abbey you'll say absolutely nothing about the concentration camp. Nothing at all. And if anyone asks—you'll tell them— you've never heard of Mauthausen. You will pretend to be Benedictine monks while you're there. And have recently come from the Archabbey of Pannonhalma in Hungary. That's Archabbey of Pannonhalma. Does everyone understand my Hungarian?" the major asked through the workers' din.

The three men acknowledged they understood.

"Are there any more questions?"

"When do we start work at the monastery?" Ben inquired.

"The day after you arrive there, Brother Benjamin. Tomorrow at four in the morning, before anyone else gets here, the three of you will come and pack your tools. I'll meet you here, and my driver will take you to Saint Clemens. Remember, not a word of this to anyone. Have a good evening, brothers. Lock your lockers. I believe it's time for roll call," the major said as a loud bell rang inside the maintenance building.

16

June 6, 1944

D-Day

In the muted darkness of Barracks 20, Ben tiredly climbed down from the top bunk while the hundred or more other prisoners slept, all except for a few who were secretively masturbating underneath their lice-ridden blankets. Ben made sure his watch was in his pocket before putting on his grubby canvas shoes. He gently shook Mr. Katz's arm, then whispered, "Get up, it's time to go, brother."

"Okay."

The two men went to the communal wash area, where Zohar was already shaving in a small handheld mirror. He raised his eyes to the men but remained silent. A naked man nearby was puking into a toilet; he gave the three men a brief glance before going back to what he was doing.

Not wanting to arouse much attention, the three prisoners exited the barracks five minutes apart. Zohar left first Ben second, and Mr. Katz last. Each of them showed their camp passes a the barely responsive kapo who was on duty by the barracks door. A Nazi guard was passed out in his chair, heavily snoring.

For some reason, the camp lights weren't on outside, including the ones in the guard towers. One by one, the three men felt their way into the dark maintenance building, only turning on the single light bulb above their workstation. They packed tools into their wooden milk crates, and by four o'clock, Major Himmel shined a flashlight through the doorway. The three men watched as the light grew brighter.

"Hurry, men. Take your boxes and follow me."

The three prisoners went outside and loaded the boxes into the trunk of the idling Mercedes. It was a foggy morning, and Ben noticed a faint blue ring of light around the automobile.

"Get in the car, brothers," the major ordered.

His driver wiped away a grayish white chimney ash from the side-view mirrors and windshield. He closed the trunk and the doors and then sat behind the wheel. The *Kübelwagen* escorted the major's vehicle through the open guard gate. The sentry there lethargically waved as the car and *Kübelwagen* sped through the sleepy village of Mauthausen. After twenty minutes, the two vehicles quietly pulled onto a dirt road and switched off their headlights. They rolled a quarter kilometer past a farmhouse and stopped shortly thereafter. The major turned on the overhead light while Raphael got out to open the rear trunk.

"The clothes you'll be wearing at the monastery are in three garment bags inside the trunk," the major said. "Your names are on the bags. Go outside and change. Put your prison uniforms and shoes into the empty garment bags, then pile them onto the side of the road. Do it fast—now."

While Ben, Zohar, and Mr. Katz put on their new clothing, a woman illuminated a porch light from the farmhouse down the road. She yelled, and a dog barked. A man came out and fired a hunting rifle.

"Hurry, men," the major said, as he got out of the car. He waited until they filled the garment bags and stacked them on the side of the road. The major felt a bullet whiz past his ear. "Get in the car—hurry."

The new monks lifted the bottoms of their black robes and climbed inside the bulletproof limo. The major opened a small jar that contained gasoline; he poured the fuel over the garment bags and struck a match to the pile. It blazed. The major got back in the car.

"Drive, Raphael."

"*Ja,* Major.*"

With their high beams shining, the vehicles swiftly turned around and drove down the dirt road. They pulled onto the highway again. Ben smelled and felt the material on the black robe he was wearing. It was smooth, clean, and comfortable, compared to the scratchy prison uniforms they left burning on the side of the dirt road.

Farther along the route, a broadcaster excitedly announced from the radio inside the blue limo. "Good morning. This is John Snagge from the BBC in London.

I've just been informed that the American, British, and Canadian airborne troops have landed on the beaches of Normandy, France, early this morning. D-day has begun! I repeat, D-day has begun!"

"Brother Benjamin," Zohar whispered. "The allies are in France."

"Oh?"

The major smiled, closed his eyes, and then took a brief nap.

* * *

The Mercedes and the military vehicle traveled a few more kilometers before entering the village of Melk. They went through the town, accelerated to the top of a steep hill, and parked by the entrance to Saint Clemens Monastery. A speck of orange-red light appeared on the horizon. The major's chauffeur stepped out and opened the trunk. He unloaded the three milk crates filled with tools, then closed the trunk and opened the back doors.

The major turned around to the back seat, "Be sure to do good work, brothers. Farewell. And may God be with you always. He made the sign of the cross, and the three men climbed from the car without saying a word. Raphael closed the doors and got behind the wheel again. Abbot Zebedee stood by the front entrance and waved to Major Himmel. He waved back. The major and his driver put on dark sunglasses, and the two vehicles headed toward the rising sun.

"Ah . . . the monks from Pannonhalma Archabbey are here. Welcome to Saint Clemens Monastery," Abbot Zebedee greeted. "Come inside, brothers. Leave your tools in the hall for now," he said. The abbot shut the thick wooden door and locked it. "My name is Abbot Zebedee. I'm in charge of the monastery. Introduce yourselves, brothers."

"I'm Brother Benjamin."

Ben and the abbot shook hands.

"You have a powerful grip, my friend. And what is your occupation, Brother Benjamin?"

"I'm a glazier."

"Good. We have many broken windows at the monastery," the abbot stated. He turned to the tallest man. "And what is your name, my friend?"

"Brother Zohar. I'm an electrician."

"Excellent. We have much electrical work that needs updating."

Zohar smiled and shook hands with the abbot.

And who are you, brother?"

"My name is Brother Jacob, Your Majesty."

"The shoemaker, I presume?"

"Yes, Your Majesty."

"I'm not a king, Brother Jacob. Just a humble abbot. I can do without the majesty."

"Yes, sir."

"I'm pleased to meet you all. We'll go to my office now and drink coffee. Come, it's right this way."

The three new monks followed the large man into his office.

"Sit," the abbot said as he poured steaming hot coffee into four cups. "How do we take our coffee?"

"Black," the three men replied in unison.

"Here—be careful—it's very hot."

The abbot opened a top drawer of his desk and took out three wood crosses on beaded necklaces. He handed each man one.

"Put these necklaces on. And only take them off when you have a bath or go to sleep. You're Jews, so wearing a cross will undoubtedly feel strange at first."

"I'm a Protestant," Brother Zohar stated.

"Good. I'll teach everyone the sign of the cross," the abbot said, proceeding to show them the movements of the ritual a few times.

The men mimicked him.

"I think you've got the hang of it. I'm certain you'll all adapt well to the customs at Saint Clemens. Just be extremely careful of what you say when you're around the other brothers and sisters. Don't mention anything about the concentration camp, especially to Prior Mueller. You'll probably meet him soon. He's my assistant at the abbey. Major Himmel may have informed you already, but if anyone asks, you've come from the Archabbey of Pannonhalma. That's Archabbey of Pannonhalma. Memorize it well, brothers. Be sure to follow how the other monks behave around here. You should be fine."

* * *

When Prior Mueller finished his early morning prayers, he closed his breviary, left the chapel, and then proceeded down the hallway toward the front vestibule. He wondered why the three milk crates filled with tools were on the floor there. Scratching his head, he knocked on Abbot Zebedee's door.

"Come in."

"Why are those milk crates in the foyer?" the prior questioned. "Oh! Good morning. I'm sorry, Abbot, didn't know you would have company this early."

"Good morning, Prior."

The three new monks were rehearsing the sign of the cross. The prior looked at them, smiled, and then returned the ritual.

"The tools belong to the three new brothers from the Archabbey of Pannonhalma. I told you about them yesterday. May I introduce you to Brother Benjamin, this is Brother Jacob, and Brother Zohar." The abbot nodded to each of them in turn.

"Welcome, brothers. I'm Prior Mueller."

They all shook hands, and the prior observed the men's exhausted faces, and felt the scrapes and calluses on their fingers and palms.

"Where will they be staying?" the prior asked.

"I prepared the three end rooms on the top floor. Give them clean towels and soap and show them where they can bathe. Afterward, you'll bring them down to breakfast. They've had an arduous journey from Hungary. I'm sure they must be famished."

"Yes, sir."

"And once they've eaten, Brother Joseph will show them where their workbenches are in the basement. He'll give them a full tour of the monastery after. I'll be up in the library if I'm needed. Have a blessed day everyone."

17

Commandant Graben turned over in bed and dreamed he was trapped inside a glass paperweight; similar to, but a much larger version of the one he had on his desk at the camp. In his underwear, he shivered while banging on the thick glass and calling for help. Snowflakes fell. Outside of the glass, three Santa Clauses laughed and waved to the commandant. A big yellow fish swam past the sleeping Nazi. The dream ended.

The commandant was abruptly awakened by Sergeant Heimlich, who was shouting into the bedroom phone. The sergeant listened for a while, then slammed down the receiver.

"What's the matter, Sergeant?"

"Corporal Wagner just informed me that a few hundred prisoners escaped from the camp last night."

"What!"

"Officers from the Russian compound and several Hungarian prisoners from Barracks 20."

"How did that happen?"

The commandant climbed out of bed and put on his bathrobe and slippers. He reached for a cigarette. "Give me a light."

"Wagner said the guards on duty this morning found holes cut into the electric fences," the sergeant replied, "Someone rigged the breaker box for the entire camp, and the power and lights went off last night. The guards in the watchtowers were found asleep early this morning. They may have been drugged."

"Drugged?"

"*Ja.* Some kind of strong sedative," the sergeant replied.

"Get me a coffee."

* * *

The sergeant and the commandant stood on the front porch of the villa, and they noticed that the military vehicle and the major's blue Mercedes were gone from the driveway.

"Our guests must be eating an early breakfast at the camp," the commandant said. "Let's see what's going on with this escape."

They got into the commandant's black Mercedes, and the sergeant rode the brake down the steep driveway.

"So, how was the meeting yesterday?" the sergeant inquired.

"Fine. Just odd the major didn't attend. I gave the other two officers and their wives a tour of the camp. Before they leave, I'll be having lunch with the major and his wife."

"Where at?"

"The *Ailes d'ange.* The major said he loves French food, so I thought I'd take them there. He wants to brief me on some plans about a super rocket the *führer's* scientists have been developing at the sub-camp near Melk."

"Gusen?"

"*Ja.* Top secret."

The sergeant approached the front guard gate and stopped. Corporal Wagner greeted the two men, focusing through his thick eyeglasses to see who they were.

"*Heil Hellmenz*, Commandant, Sergeant."

"*Ya.* Any news about the escaped prisoners?" the commandant inquired.

"Several were found dead outside the camp's perimeter," the corporal replied. "The mayor of Mauthausen called five minutes ago. He said a large group of prisoners were wandering around the village, looking for food and water."

"Have you seen Major Himmel and his group?"

"*Nein*, Commandant."

"Let's go, Sergeant."

They drove into the camp and parked next to a rusted blue motorcycle with a sidecar attached. The two men got out and stared at the vehicle.

"Who does that belong to?" the commandant asked.

"I don't know . . . I've never seen it here before."

"Strange," the commandant stated. "I want you to form a work crew, Heimlich. Have them collect the prisoners who died by the camp's perimeter. Burn the bodies. Get a manhunt organized immediately. Contact Mayor Fickmich in Mauthausen and tell him to recruit a large group of men—the youth brigade can join them as well. We'll need tracking dogs too. After roll call, I want every god-damn prisoner stripped naked and moved to the garage yard. Have a firing squad shoot the remaining prisoners from Barracks 20 and the Russian compound."

* * *

Like a crazed Nazi, Sergeant Heimlich swung his arms up and down and high-stepped into the maintenance building. He stomped over to the shoemaker's workbench and noticed that his tool locker had been left open. All the tools and some shoe leather had been taken. A lone shoehorn and Mr. Katz's yellow work pass was left behind. The angry sergeant inspected the electrician's work area next. It was a mess. Wires were everywhere, the locker open, everything missing, except for a powerful hand tool used to cut through metal fences like butter. Zohar's work pass had been taped to his locker, and he had drawn a caricature of the *Fuhrer's* rabid looking face on the work pass. At Ben's well-organized worktable, the sergeant picked up the empty box the glass cutters had come in. He looked inside the glazier's locker and found that it was emptied also. The sergeant kicked over a mirror and asked a Spanish welder if he had seen anything unusual the last couple of days.

"*Nein*, Sergeant."

The welder smiled, pursed his lips, and then returned to work.

* * *

The commandant saw that the dignitaries from Berlin were not inside the officers dining room. He stormed over to the administration building, then entered his secretary's office. She was in the middle of nonchalantly painting her toenails black and red.

"There was an escape last night," she said without looking up from her toenails.

"I already heard. Any mail or telegrams, Mrs. Holstein?"

"*Nein,* but someone left a package by your door."

"Who is it from?"

"I don't know," she impudently replied. "It was here when I arrived this morning."

"Have you seen Major Himmel, or the other officers?"

"Nein."

"He and his wife will be coming in today," the commandant announced. "I'll need you to make a good impression. Try to look presentable. Okay, Mrs. Holstein?"

"Jawohl."

"And I hope you remembered to put your underpants on this morning, Mrs. Holstein."

"Yes, Commandant, I have. They're black and made out of silk. Would you like to see them?"

"That won't be necessary. What's that scent you're wearing?" he asked, sniffing the sweetly perfumed air.

"Patchouli. Do you like it?"

"It's nice. A bit on the heavy side."

The commandant left his secretary's office and stopped by his door to pick up the package on the floor. He brought it inside, set it on his desk, and pulled out a bottle of Benedictine and Brandy. He read a note that was attached.

Dear Commandant Graben,

This is a small token of our appreciation

for your generous hospitality.

I'm sorry to inform you, but due to unforeseen

circumstances, I must cancel our luncheon for today.

The other officers and I were summoned

back to Berlin immediately.

Best wishes,

Major Wolfgang Himmel

Office of the High Command in Berlin

Sergeant Heimlich rushed into the commandant's office. "I have some more bad news."

"What is it now, Sergeant?"

"The glazier, the shoemaker, and the electrician must have escaped last night. They weren't at roll call this morning."

"Have you checked the maintenance building?"

"They're not there either. And their tools are missing."

"*Schweinhunds!*" the commandant shouted, crumpling the major's note in his hand. "Is that group for the manhunt ready?"

"Almost. I spoke with Mayor Fickmich ten minutes ago. I'll be going with them."

"*Gut.* Be sure to search every house and farm in the area. I want those prisoners hunted down and butchered like pigs, Heimlich. Understand?"

"*Ja.* Who gave you the gift?" the sergeant asked, noticing the bottle of Benedictine and Brandy on the desk.

"The major! Now get that fucking manhunt organized, or you'll be working in the quarry today."

After the sergeant left the office, the commandant angrily lit a cigarette and picked up and shook his heavy glass paperweight. He observed the miniature winter landscape, then suddenly recalled the bizarre dream he had last night. He flung the heavy object across the room, and it busted the glass on his aquarium. The water gushed out, taking the tropical fish with it.

In the pandemonium filled town hall of Mauthausen: soldiers, thirty boys from the Nazi youth movement, a few dozen concerned Austrian locals, and several farmers with their older sons, gathered with their military weapons, hunting rifles, pistols, machetes, axes, pitchforks, and wooden clubs. Outside, twenty-five cigarette-smoking Gestapo held vigil while restraining their leashed, sharp-teethed, and salivating bloodhounds and shepherds.

Sergeant Heimlich signaled to the large group inside the town hall, and the raucous mob burst through the doorway. They zealously marched and drove vehicles through the town square. The corpulent mayor and the sheriff of Mauthausen remained behind at the town hall, stuffing themselves with a breakfast of sweet pastries and goose liver. Afterward, they washed it down with a frothy German lager.

* * *

A military vehicle drove around the village of Mauthausen while a loudspeaker blared from its roof: "The escaped prisoners are armed and dangerous criminals. Do not to go near, feed, give shelter, or help the criminals in any manner whatsoever," a soldier on the loudspeaker announced. "Anyone found aiding the escaped prisoners will suffer dire consequences."

The military vehicle drove onto another street, and the loudspeaker broadcasted the same message.

* * *

Sergeant Heimlich and an SS officer commandeered the manhunt from a *Kübelwagen*. Riding in cars, motorcycles, and on the backs of army trucks. The riotous mob swiftly discovered a couple dozen escapees who were staggering and limping aimlessly throughout the innocent village. The hungry hatchet-faced prisoners were found slumped on stoops, park benches, street curbs, in front of shops, and beside the tracks at the Mauthausen train station. The riotous mob slaughtered the pajama-dressed men where they rested. The hundred or more members on the manhunt broke off into splinter groups, and the bloodletting search proceeded to the next locale.

* * *

At a dairy farm right outside the town, a soldier smashed his gloved fist on a farmhouse door while a few Nazi youths investigated the property and barn.

"Open the door!" the soldier yelled.

The farmer's wife appeared, dressed in coveralls and kitchen apron. She had a frightened look on her face. "Can I help you?" she asked the young soldier.

"We're looking for the prisoners who escaped from Mauthausen last night. Are any of the killers here?" he asked, peering through the doorway.

"Killers? Of course not. We have no killers here."

The soldier ogled the farmer's wife. "You're a beautiful woman."

"I'm married," she said, showing him her ring.

"I'm hungry and give me coffee!" the unwelcome soldier ordered as he barged into the home. The woman showed him where the kitchen was, and he sat at the table. She made a pot of fresh coffee, sliced some bread, and boiled some eggs. The soldier's cigarette smoke stank up the room. He asked, "And, where is your husband, pretty woman?"

"Working."

The farmer finished milking his cows and tiredly walked into the house. Coughing from the tobacco smoke, he was shocked to see a Nazi soldier sitting at his kitchen table, flirting with his wife, and gobbling down hard-boiled eggs and buttered bread.

"What are these people doing here, Elsa?" the farmer asked his wife.

"He insisted on coming in."

The soldier regurgitated some egg white. "Silence!" he yelled. "The Jewish murderers are everywhere.

They're armed and dangerous. We must search your house."

"This is a farm," the husband stated. "We have no murderers here. Please remove yourself from my house."

"Shut up! We shall see," the young Nazi said while getting up from the table.

The farmer's wife put her hand over her mouth in fear. The soldier stomped upstairs, where he found three of their children and grandparents shaking in their beds. Three teenage Nazi youths came inside and searched the basement. It didn't take long for them to discover two men cowering underneath some dirt in a root cellar. The youths pulled them out and led them upstairs.

"What do we have here?" the soldier questioned. "I thought you said there wasn't anyone in the house. You lied!"

The farmer's wife's heart sank when she noticed the yellow Jewish stars sewn onto the men's shirts.

"Protecting Jews is serious a crime," the soldier said.

"We didn't know they were here—they must have come into the house last night," the farmer's wife explained. "While we were sleeping. We didn't hear anyone."

"And we never lock our doors," the Austrian farmer added.

"No? I don't believe you!" the soldier exclaimed. "You and your family are under arrest for harboring escaped prisoners."

"Our family? Honestly. Please. We didn't know they were down there," the farmer pleaded in vain.

"Take the two prisoners outside and shoot them," the Gestapo ordered the Nazi youth. "You go with them," the farmer was told.

"*Jawohl, Capitan,*" the older of the three boys said. "*Rouse, Juden.*"

When they left, the young soldier grabbed the farmer's wife by the hand; he took her upstairs, and then raped her in the master bedroom. Afterward, the entire family was taken away to the concentration camp down the road.

* * *

The manhunt moved on to the next farmhouse and village. Bloodthirsty dogs tracked the scent of escaped prisoners, leading the mobs through the forest. They hunted the men past sundown, through the night, and into the following day. The majority of them had been rounded up and killed. Less than a dozen escaped capture. More than two hundred were left dead on the roadsides, farms, streets of the quaint Austrian villages and throughout the surrounding woods. For two days, camp prisoners, farmers, and the people of the towns loaded the emaciated corpses onto long trucks and wagons. The dead were transported to empty fields, where earth-digging vehicles hollowed out long burial trenches. Trucks delivered the rest of the corpses back to Mauthausen's sub-camps, where they were burned in the ovens.

* * *

Back at his private villa, Commandant Graben poured some Benedictine and Brandy into three glasses. He handed one to an exhausted Sergeant Heimlich, and one to the SS officer who had been in charge of the manhunt. The three Nazis raised their glasses.

"To a job well done, gentlemen," the commandant toasted.

"*Danke schön. Prost.*"

"*Prost.*"

The three men drank up and laughed. The lavishly decorated bar filled with a foggy thick cigar smoke.

"Did you find all of the escaped prisoners, Franz?" the commandant asked the SS officer.

"*Nein.* We killed most of the Russian officers, except for six or seven we couldn't locate. Three Hungarian prisoners from Barracks 20 are still unaccounted for."

"Who are they?" the commandant curiously inquired.

Franz read from a list of names, "prisoners Zugreb, Katz, and Weiss."

"Keep looking for them. When you find these three prisoners, bring them back to me alive. I will castrate them myself."

"*Jawohl.*"

The commandant angrily jabbed a long sharp knife into the bar. He picked up the bottle of Benedictine and Brandy and refilled the three glasses.

19

Almost to the end of his first day at the monastery, Ben meditated by a quickening twilight in the chapel. A turtle dove startled him by crazily flying in circles directly above his head. He flailed his arms, attempting to shoo away the creature. An elderly monk stood by and clapped his hands twice; the fine-feathered friend spiraled up toward a broken stained-glass window, where it softly cooed.

"They're harmless. Although annoying," the older monk said, offering to shake Ben's hand. "I'm Brother Zebulon. You must be the new monk in town."

"I am. Brother Benjamin."

"Where ya from, brother?"

"Hungary. The Archabbey of Pannonhalma."

"It's nice meeting you, brother. Have a peaceful evening."

"You, as well."

Ben sat again, looked above, and continued with his thoughts. He wondered about his mother and father's whereabouts, as well as that of his siblings. He missed them all. *Papa wouldn't have endured a single day's work at Mauthausen, and no women there were Mama's age. Maybe they were taken somewhere else.* Ben didn't want to think the worst. Not knowing really troubled him. Even though he was gone from the camp, his heart filled with a melancholy. A sister entered the shadowy chapel, and she lit some votive candles on a credenza by the large oak doors. He looked at the light, and the sister noticed his worried disposition. More monks and sisters entered the chapel. Brother Jacob tapped on Ben's shoulder, and he sat on his right side, while Brother Zohar sat on his left. Vespers (evening prayers) had begun.

After praying, the three new monks departed the chapel and climbed the staircase to the third floor. They bid each other a good night, and Ben opened the door to his tiny room. A moonlight stared in from a large window. He struck a wooden match and lit the wick inside of an oil lamp on a small desk. Ben sat by it, noticing a pen, paper, and a note with someone's handwriting.

Dear Brother Benjamin,

Welcome to Saint Clemens Monastery. We wish

your stay here only be filled with blessings and joy.

Sincerely,

Abbot Zebedee and all the brothers and sisters

Ben's heart uplifted somewhat after reading the kind message. He opened his pocket watch, put it near the light, and saw that it was eight o'clock. It was nothing short of a miracle he still owned it. He undressed and removed the cross from around his neck. After extinguishing the lamp flame, the new monk sat on the small but comfortable bed. The first one he would be sleeping in since leaving Beregszász.

* * *

In the distance, sounds of bombing and air-raid sirens disturbed Ben's deep sleep. He opened his eyes and prayed. It was dark outside. He got out of bed and lit the lamp on the desk. He dressed, put on the necklace, and opened his watch; the hour was five o'clock. He placed the watch in a pocket of his robe, put on his shoes, and then hurried to the bathroom at the end of the hall.

When Ben returned to the room, Zohar was standing by his door, tall, dignified and dressed in his lengthy black monk's robe. Ben thought the religious apparel suited him well.

"Good morning, Brother Zohar."

"Morning, Ben . . . I have some good news for you."

"Come in for a minute. We can talk inside."

While Ben made his bed, Zohar peered at himself in the mirror. A framed portrait of Christ hung beside it.

"How do you like your room, Ben? Mine feels kind of small."

"That's because you're so tall—what about the good news?"

"The American and British forces have advanced. They've succeeded in breaching Germany's coastal defense of France. Not without casualties, unfortunately. A few thousand allied soldiers died."

"Oh." Ben tied his shoelaces and asked, "Who told you that?"

"I heard it on the BBC last night. The station came in loud and clear."

"From the radio in the dining room?"

"No. On the commandant's short-wave radio," Zohar replied. "I packed it in the milk crate by mistake. I finally fixed it last night."

"Don't let anyone know you have it, or we'll all be in trouble."

"I keep the volume down low. And I have a good hiding place for it."

"Be careful just the same."

"I will. Are you ready to go downstairs for prayers?" Zohar asked.

"Let's see if Brother Jacob is awake first."

20

After prayers and breakfast, Ben sat on a bench under a birch tree in the cloister. He checked the time; it was half-past seven. He left the open watch beside him, read from the Book of Psalms. Chapter 23, verse 3. "He restores my soul. He leads me in the paths of righteousness for His name's sake."

A blue bird sang in the tree branches above him while a fellow monk passed by with a bucket of hot soapy water; the monk set the bucket down and started scrubbing a life-size statue of Saint Francis, the patron saint of animals.

Ben closed his eyes and flashed back to the time he was a small boy. He was riding with his father on the horse-drawn wagon, delivering a Christmas tree in Beregszász. They stopped in front of a church, and the young horse snorted into the freezing white air. Little Ben watched, as the priest and his father pulled a large fragrant evergreen off the wagon and haul it inside the church. He followed them inside, inhaling a sweet-smelling incense. The priest paid Mr. Weiss, then handed Ben a peppermint candy cane and gently patted his head.

He fondly remembered, then resumed reading Psalms, chapter 23, verse 5. "You prepare a table before me in the presence of my enemies. You anoint my head with oil, my cup overflows."

Prior Mueller entered the cloister, and he walked over to where Ben was praying.

"Good morning, brother."

"Morning, Prior."

Ben made the sign of the cross, closed the Bible, and then looked up at the prior and smiled.

"Getting acquainted with your new surroundings, I see," the prior said, noticing the gold-plated pocket watch on the bench.

"It's nice to sit out here," Ben said. "Peaceful."

"What time is it?"

Ben reached into his robe pocket, forgetting that he had left the watch on the bench.

"There it is," the prior said, pointing.

"Oh . . . it's almost eight."

"That's a nice watch—where did you get it from?"

"My father gave it to me."

"Can I see it?"

Ben handed him the watch, and the prior carefully examined it. "Whoever made this did excellent workmanship. Does your father live in Hungary?"

The prior reluctantly handed Ben the watch.

"I don't know where my father is."

"And your mother?"

"I don't know where she is either."

"I'm sorry—I shouldn't be so meddlesome. If you're ready, brother, I'll show you where you'll be working today."

"Oh."

Ben put the watch in his pocket and grasped the handle on a small toolbox by his feet. They left the cloister and headed toward the main annex of the abbey. The prior stopped when he felt a draft coming through the chapel doors. He closed them and turned to Ben.

"A few of the stained-glass windows are broken inside the chapel," the prior said. "They'll need to be replaced eventually. Gets too drafty. And the damn birds keep flying in and make an awful mess. I hate birds. Bothersome creatures. Wonder why God ever created them."

"How did the windows break?"

"Bombing from the American and British Air Forces," the prior snarled. "Shame the Luftwaffe can't blow them out of the sky more often."

"I should repair the windows before the winter sets in. Don't you think?"

"I'd have to ask the abbot first. Stained glass is expensive. And probably difficult, if not near impossible to find right now. You'll have plenty more windows to fix in the sisters' dormitory. We're going there now."

The two men climbed the stairs to the second floor. At the end of a hallway, a noticeable odor blew in through a large open window. The prior coughed into his handkerchief.

"Smell that?" the prior inquired. "You should with that large nose of yours."

The prior chuckled behind his handkerchief.

Ben didn't like his humor much. "Oh—what is it?" he asked, stiffening his muscular shoulder blades.

"It's from the concentration camp down the road. Mauthausen. They burn dead bodies there. Mostly Jews."

"Oh, that's a terrible smell," Ben said, covering his nose and mouth with his hand.

"It is, indeed. That's how the Nazis get rid of the prisoners who aren't working hard enough," the prior once again calmly stated.

"By burning them?"

"*Ja.*"

"Oh."

"You say that often," the prior said. "Why is that?"

"Say what?" Ben asked.

"*Oh.*"

"It's just a funny habit of mine." Ben replied.

"Habits can be broken, brother."

Ben thought to himself. Like burning dead Jews?

"What's the matter, brother? You looked as if you wanted to say something."

"I did. Where are you from, Prior Mueller?"

"Nuremberg. Know where that is?"

"It's a city in Germany."

"You know your geography. Have you been there?"

"Never. I studied the countries of Europe at the Archabbey of Pannonhalma."

"*Wunderbar.* Enough of the small talk," the prior said. "The sisters' rooms are on this floor." The two men stood in front of a door. "The brothers are seldom allowed up here, unless they have special permission from me or Abbot Zebedee. This is Sister Hildegard's room. Pardon her. She behaves a little strange sometimes."

"Oh?"

"She's the head baker at the monastery."

The prior knocked, and they waited several moments till a nun opened the door halfway. A young, blue-eyed woman smiled as she inquisitively looked at the men standing in the hallway. An abundance of wavy blond locks hung past her shoulders. Ben was awestruck by the sister's profound beauty.

"What is it, Prior?" she asked, momentarily gazing into Ben's deep, hazel-green eyes.

"Pardon the intrusion, Sister Hildegard. This is Brother Benjamin. He's one of the new monks who's come from the Archabbey of Pannonhalma."

"Yes. In Hungary. Abbot Zebedee mentioned something about it," the sister said.

"Brother Benjamin will be repairing the broken windows at the monastery. He speaks Hungarian, but he knows German quite well. And a little English."

"Welcome, brother," the sister greeted in Hungarian.

"Thank you. It's a pleasure to meet you, sister."

"Likewise."

"If it's not too much of an inconvenience, Brother Benjamin will repair your window today," the prior said.

"I'm delighted it's finally going to be fixed," she said. "Been broken since the war started. Come in, brothers."

The men followed Sister Hildegarde inside, and she walked over to the only window in the room: a large, wood-framed window with four separate panes. Three of the panes were missing; weathered cardboard had been barricaded there instead.

"That's it, brother," she told Ben.

The prior sneezed from the incense that burned from a hanging metal censer nearby. He looked critically at the sister's display of wavy blond hair, not approving of her rose-colored lipstick either.

"I believe it's time for a haircut, Sister Hildegard," the prior announced. "And what's that red stuff on your lips?"

"I can manage my own affairs, thank you," she said, giving the judgmental prior a reproachful glance. The attractive nun gathered her hair into a bun, attached a clip, and then yanked a hood over her head. She wiped her lips with a cloth. "That beard of yours could use a trim, Prior," she said in a rather brusque manner.

His pale-skinned nose and cheeks flushed with embarrassment. He sniffled some. And sneezed again.

"I'll leave you to your work now, brother," the prior said. "If you need anything, I'll be in Abbot Zebedee's office."

"Prior?" the sister asked.

"*Ja?*"

"Would you kindly burn some incense in the hall. It's beginning to smell like death out there. Leave the censer on the hook when you're done."

Ben opened the toolbox, took out a ruler, and measured the window frame. He jotted down the dimensions on a piece of scrap paper. In the meantime, Sister Hildegard removed her hood and released the hair clip, allowing her full head of sun-bleached locks to hang free again. She reapplied more rose-colored lipstick, then puckered her lips.

"He can be quite a nuisance sometimes," the sister stated.

"Who is that?"

"Prior Mueller."

"Oh."

The sister watched as Ben scraped the hardened putty and jagged bits of glass from the frame's edges.

"You can put that in here," she said, handing him a small cardboard box.

After cleaning the window frame, Ben swept the mess into the box, then rested in front of the open window. He had worked up a sweat. Sister Hildegard handed him a glass of water.

"Thank you."

"You're welcome. There's that terrible odor again," she said while crinkling her nose. "It's from the camp down the road. I'll have to burn more incense in here. I know you've only been at the monastery a short time, brother. But how are you finding Saint Clemens?"

"It's a very pleasant monastery. And the other brothers and sisters have been extremely helpful to us."

"You mean your two friends?"

"*Igen.* Prior Mueller told me that you're the head baker here."

"I am."

Ben started to say, but stopped abruptly, "The bread at the monastery is far better than the concen—"

"You mean the Archabbey of Pannonhalma?" the sister asked, looking at her face from a handheld mirror.

"*Igen.*"

"Abbot Zebedee told me where you and the other two brothers have *really* come from."

"He did?"

"Mauthausen. And I know you're a Jew. Don't fret, brother—I wouldn't tell a soul—just remember what the abbot said regarding Prior Mueller. Be careful what you say to him."

"Of course."

The attractive sister moved closer to Ben. "Do you like the color of my lipstick?"

"I do. It's a pretty shade of red."

"I'm not allowed to wear it outside the room. Abbot Zebedee doesn't mind sometimes, but the prior pitches a fit if I do."

"Oh."

Sister Hildegard moved closer to Ben and stood face to face with him now, and he smelled a pleasant fragrance of spices on her clothing. She looked deep into his eyes, and he felt a spark of electricity, just as she came close enough to kiss him on the lips. She suddenly turned away and glanced toward the open window.

"There's that horrible smell again," she said.

"I'll go downstairs to the basement and cut some glass. I won't be long."

"When you return, brother, you don't have to knock. Just come in—I'll be expecting you."

"All right."

Downstairs at his workbench, Ben cut three measured pieces of glass, crumpled a page of old newspaper, and then cleaned the panes with ammonia. The glass gleamed like new afterward. Pleased with his work, the glazier wrapped the three panes in newspaper before turning off the light above his worktable. Ben left the basement and climbed the staircase to the third floor. He hastened down the hall, stopping in front of Sister Hildegard's door; he was about to knock when he remembered what she had told him before he left for the basement. He turned the black knob and pushed the door open. As he entered the room, a thick, purplish-blue cloud of sweet-smelling frankincense enveloped him; it was almost overwhelming. He coughed. Meanwhile, a mysterious violet light poured in through the broken window.

"I'm back, Sister Hildegard."

Ben heard the sister speak, but not from inside the room; her voice sounded as if it carried in on a breeze outside the window: "Brother . . . I didn't think you'd be returning that fast."

"Is that you, Sister?"

"*Igen.*"

When the incense smoke dissipated, Brother Benjamin saw that Sister Hildegard was standing undressed; her backside faced him, and a violet aura surrounded her nude sunlit body. Ben was so transfixed he was unable to speak, move, or breathe. He wanted to leave the room, but his shoes seemed as if they were well-glued to the floor. Ben trembled as an awesome fear came over him. He separated from his physical body, and his spirit rose. Touching the ceiling with his hand, he clearly saw that the sister's wavy blond hair dripped wet and hung all the way down her backside. Beads of moisture made her skin glow. Attached to the sister's bare shoulder blades, Ben thought he saw what looked like a pair of glistening gold wings etched with white on their tips. He had never seen anything more terrifying yet beautiful in his entire life.

"Oh, my God!" he exclaimed. The violet light bedazzled him.

"Don't be afraid, brother."

Ben felt a strong yet gentle pull. And his feet became planted inside his shoes again. He looked upon the sister's bare shoulders, but the gold wings were gone.

She spoke in a matter-of-fact tone, "I just came back from a shower. Step out of the room, brother. I'll only be a few minutes."

Ben's feet weighed heavy as he moved one and then the other. He stuttered an apology before leaving the room. Inside the hallway, he kept his balance by holding his free hand against the wall. He was dizzy. His mind reeled from what he had seen—*what he thought he had seen.* Not knowing whether to believe it or not, Ben pinched himself to see if he was dreaming. A sister stopped when she noticed the monk awkwardly standing there, holding the glass wrapped in newspaper and bracing himself against the wall.

"Can I help you, brother? Are you lost?" she asked, snapping her thumb and forefinger.

"Who are you?" Ben asked as though he had just awakened from a deep slumber.

"Sister Saint Andrews—I'm the prioress at Saint Clemens. Monks aren't allowed on this floor. Are you all right, brother?"

"I felt a little dizzy before. I'm fine. It's because of that awful smell."

"Yes—it's horrendous today," the sister said. "Why don't you sit on this chair and rest a few moments?"

Ben was still confused by what had transpired in Sister Hildegard's room.

"I haven't seen you at the monastery until now," the nun said. "What's your name?"

Ben almost forgot. He remembered about the panes of glass that were tucked under his arm.

"I'm Brother Benjamin. I'm working up here, today."

"That's right. Abbot Zebedee mentioned it at breakfast. You're one of the new monks from Hungary. Welcome. What kind of work do you do, Brother Benjamin?"

"I fix broken windows."

"*Wunderbar.* Perhaps you could repair my window today," Sister Saint Andrews said. "There's a terrible draft inside my room."

"I'd be happy to. As soon as I'm done with—"

"Brother Benjamin?" Sister Hildegard called from the threshold of her doorway down the hall.

"*Igen?*"

"You can finish your work now."

21

Abbot Zebedee peered through his office window while a squadron of American B-17 bombers roared in the skies over the monastery, vibrating framed pictures, and rattling teacups and spoons atop a coffee table.

"There they are again," the abbot mentioned as he caught the tail end of the flying fortress. "I hope it's the allies this time. Prior, why don't you heat up some more water in the kettle, please."

"*Jawohl*, commandant."

The prior smirked, clicked his heels together, and then gave the abbot a tall Nazi salute.

"That's not funny, Mueller. Not funny at all."

Sister Hildegard came down the hallway with a plate of freshly baked blackberry scones. She stopped in front of the abbot's door and knocked.

"Enter."

"Morning, brothers."

"Good morning, Sister Hildegarde," the abbot greeted, eying the delectable-looking pastries she had on the plate.

"Brought you some blackberry scones—still warm from the oven—thought they'd go well with your tea this morning," the sister said, handing him the plate.

"Oh, they smell wonderful!" the abbot declared. "Thank you, sister. Joining us?"

"I would, but I have bread in the oven. Enjoy the scones."

"God bless," the abbot said. "And thanks again."

"You're welcome."

She left, and the abbot chose a scone off the plate and inhaled the fresh-baked aroma. He took a bite. Then another.

"Would you care for one, Prior? They are delicious," the abbot asked, as his assistant turned off the gas flame under the tea kettle.

"No, thanks. I don't like the taste of blackberries."

"That's where we differ. Happens to be my favorite berry. Especially love them in pie. Yum. Nothing like a good blackberry pie."

"Try not to eat them all in one sitting," the prior said, pouring more steaming water into their cups.

"Please. Spare me the advice, Prior."

"I really find it strange how those three new monks came here in the middle of a war," the prior stated. "Rather dangerous in my opinion."

"Are you questioning the Lord's actions, Prior? Nothing is too dangerous as far as God is concerned. And I certainly have no qualms regarding the brothers. They're diligent workers, keep to the prayer schedule, and haven't caused us any problems so far."

"I suppose you're right."

"*Suppose,* Prior?"

"Brother Zohar looks like a good Christian man, but the other two monks seem different," Prior Mueller said.

"How so?"

"Their noses are bigger than the average gentile's nose."

The abbot laughed.

"That's absurd, Prior. Big noses? Look at my nose. It's a large Roman nose. But why would you think someone's facial features, or the size of their nose have anything to do with being a monk? Plenty of brothers and sisters around here have long noses. And they aren't Jews."

"That's true," the prior said. "It's completely irrelevant."

"Of course, it is—you're being utterly ridiculous."

"I'll be up in the library if you need me, Abbot. Afterwards, I have to run a few errands in town. The monastery is getting low on light bulbs, soap, and toilet paper. And Sister Hildegard requested some baking supplies. Can you think of anything else we need?"

"Mint flavored chewing gum," the abbot replied. "And a carton of cigarettes. Non-filtered, please. Fill up the gas tank also. Here—you'll need some money—and don't forget the receipts.

* * *

The prior slowly climbed the vertiginous spiral staircase to the library. He reached the top floor and approached the librarian's desk.

"Morning, Prior Mueller," the librarian softly spoke, glancing up from his book.

"Good morning, Brother Martin. When you get the chance, I'll need the mailing address of Pannonhalma Archabbey. And the name of the abbot there. Believe it's located somewhere in Hungary."

"It is. Pannonhalma happens to be the second oldest Benedictine monastery in the world. It was founded in the year 996. I once visited . . ."

The prior interrupted, "Thank you for the history lesson, Brother Martin, but all I need is the abbot's name and the mailing address of the monastery. I'll be at my table when you find it."

"Yes, Prior. I'll check on it now."

"Good."

The librarian leafed through the pages of a thick yellow book; he stopped at a section, scribbled a number, and then closed the book. He sharpened a pencil then placed a phone call. The librarian conversed with someone as he wrote some information on an index card. He hung up the receiver and went over to where the prior was sitting.

"Here's what you requested, Prior."

"*Wunderbar,* Brother Martin. Good work. Come and have a glass of wine with me later this evening if you desire."

"I might just do that."

The librarian went about dusting and straightening a row of books, while the prior read the information on the index card he was given. He stroked his bearded chin and thought for a couple of minutes, dreamily gazing out a picturesque window. A packed barge slowly drifted along the Danube below. The prior picked up his ink pen and composed a letter:

Dear Abbot Cooper,

Greetings from Saint Clemens Monastery.

I hope everyone at Pannonhalma is doing well

through these most difficult times.

Abbot Zebedee and I are grateful you sent us

those three new monks. They are well-behaved and hard

workers. If there's anything I can do for you,

don't hesitate to ask.

God bless and enjoy the Benedictine and Brandy.

Sincerely Yours,

Prior Wilhelm Mueller

Saint Clemens Monastery

The prior left the library and descended the long spiral staircase. He headed for the wine cellar, where he selected a bottle then quickly went upstairs to his office. He arranged a thick bed of old newspaper into a cardboard box, placing the bottle and the envelope inside. He secured the box with tape, wrote FRAGILE GLASS, the return address, and the mailing address of Pannonhalma Archabbey on the front of the package. The prior left his office and drove the monastery's blue Mercedes to the post office in Melk. Afterward, he ran his other errands.

A mail carrier stopped at the Archabbey of Pannonhalma, and an old monk received a package and carried it down to Abbot Costello's office.

"You got mail, Abbot," the old monk announced as he poked his funny-looking head inside the doorway.

"Thank you, Brother Belluci. Leave it on the bench. And may God bless you always."

The old monk muttered a goodbye and returned to his little station near the front door.

While the warm sun rose higher on the horizon, Abbot Costello cut open the box and removed an envelope and a dark liquor bottle swaddled in newspaper. He read the label on it: *Benedictine and Brandy. Made by monks at Saint Clemens Monastery. That's weird*, he thought. The short and stocky abbot looked up and viewed the colorful Hungarian countryside through his office window. He reached for a brandy snifter on a shelf, then opened the bottle and poured himself a taste. He put down the glass, unsealed the envelope, and read the letter inside:

Dear Abbot Cooper,

Greetings from Saint Clemens Monastery I hope you and your community at Pannonhalma Archabbey are doing well through these most difficult times. Abbot Zebedee and I are grateful you sent us those three new monks . . .

Abbot Costello finished reading the letter, and he perplexedly scratched his head. *What three new monks is this Mueller character talking about?* Before the chubby little abbot of Pannonhalma sent Prior Mueller a telegram, he poured himself another drink and relaxed by the sunlit window in his office.

* * *

Back at Saint Clemens, Brother Benjamin swept his work area before supper. He darkened the light over his worktable and hurried up the stairs to the dining hall. Brothers Jacob and Zohar had saved him a place at the monks' long, smoothly polished wood table. Abbot Zebedee and Prior Mueller sat a few seats away from the three brothers. The head baker and her assistants set baskets of heavenly smelling bread onto the brothers' and sisters' tables, while cooks carried in deep tureens filled with steaming-hot bean soup, platters of baked fish, and bottles of chilled white wine. Everyone bowed their heads and gave thanks.

While they enjoyed their baked Danube salmon, Zohar nudged Ben's side with the pointy end of his elbow. "The bread here is much better than those dreadful hard rolls they served us in the camp, hah, glazier?"

The prior suspiciously turned his head toward the three Hungarian monks.

"Careful what you say, brother," Ben whispered, as the prior shot them another questioning glance.

"Sorry, I forgot," Brother Zohar said. "How's your work going in the sisters' dormitory?"

"Fine. Plenty of broken windows to repair. Where are you working?"

"I'm rigging up some new lights on the outside of the monastery," the electrician replied.

"How's that going?"

"Good."

Prior Mueller appeared annoyed, while he picked a small bone out of his fish and showed it to Abbot Zebedee.

"Look what I found."

"It's only a little bone."

"My fish seems a bit dry today," the prior said.

"Like your humor? Why can't we ever have a meal without you complaining about the food?"

The prior frowned as he placed the fish bone aside.

A monk approached the table and interrupted the two men.

"Excuse me, Prior. A telegram just came for you."

"*Danke schön.*"

The prior put down his fork and knife and put on his reading glasses. He unfolded the telegram.

"Let's hear it, then," Abbot Zebedee said.

"Sent on July 25, 1944, 3:30 p.m., from Pannonhalma Archabbey.

Dear Prior Mueller,

I'm overjoyed to hear that your three new monks are doing well at Saint Clemens, but I've only recently taken over the abbot's position here at Pannonhalma, and those three brothers you mentioned must have been sent while Abbot Cooper was still in charge of the monastery. I've never met the monks myself, and the brothers and sisters here have no recollection of them either. Unfortunately, Abbot Cooper had some health issues and passed away shortly before I arrived. He would have been the go-to person with the most knowledge about this matter. The monks may have come from another monastery altogether. Perhaps you made a mistake. Regardless, stay safe and may the good Lord bless you all at Saint Clemens. Fond regards to my good friend Abbot Zebedee, happy holidays, and thank you very much for the Benedictine and Brandy.

Sincerely yours,

Abbot Costello

The Archabbey of Pannonhalma"

Befuddled by what he had just read, the prior folded the telegram and rubbed his blond-bearded chin. He drank some wine. "That's extremely odd," he mentioned.

"What?" Abbot Zebedee asked.

"That the abbot or anyone else at Pannonhalma doesn't have any recollection of these three new brothers."

"Oh well. It was thoughtful of you to send Abbot Costello a gift," Abbot Zebedee said. "I remember him well from the seminary in Rome. The pudgy little wise guy used to sit at the desk behind me. He loved to crack jokes and play tricks on me. All in good fun. Do me a big favor, Prior, and take my plate to the kitchen. If I'm needed, I'll be digesting my food out in the cloister—it's such a lovely day out."

"Yes, sir."

The large man stood and slowly departed the dining hall.

The prior silently read the telegram once more; before placing it inside his robe pocket, he judiciously watched the three new monks rise from the supper table and bring their plates to be washed. The prior had another glass of wine, while a ray of late afternoon sunlight burned through a dining room window.

* * *

Sister Hildegard hoisted a heavy sack of pastry flour onto her shoulder, and she exited the dry goods storeroom in the basement. She was about to carry the sack up the basement steps when Prior Mueller bumped into her at the bottom of the staircase.

"Pardon me, sister."

"Prior . . . would you kindly take this flour to the bakery for me, please. I'm feeling a little weak today."

"*Ja,* of course."

Sidetracked from his original intentions of interrogating the shoemaker, the prior lifted the thirty-five-kilo bag off the sister's shoulder and placed it onto his own.

"Use the wagon after you climb the stairs," the head baker said. "I left it in the hallway. Thank you, Prior. Drop the sack by the large mixer, please. And God bless."

"*Ja,*" he grunted under the heavy weight.

The prior was out of breath after climbing the flight of stairs. Someone had taken away the wagon, so he had to schlep the heavy sack of pastry flour through the long hallway, resting twice before he finally reached the bakery. By then he had forgotten all about his plans to question the shoemaker. Completely exhausted, the prior retired to his room and had himself a lengthy nap before evening prayers.

A strong leathery odor filled the musty air around the shoemaker's workbench while he sewed a zipper onto a tall brown dress boot. Brother Jacob was so engrossed in his work; he was unaware that someone had been watching him a few moments.

"Those are lovely boots. I don't believe we've met, I'm Sister Hildegard. I work in the bakery."

The shoemaker glanced up suddenly.

"Sorry . . . I didn't mean to startle you."

"It's all right. I'm Brother Jacob."

The sister offered him a stick of chewing gum.

"Thank you."

"It's a pleasure to meet you, brother. May I sit and watch you work?" she asked, brushing some flour off her apron.

"Be my guest."

"I met your friend, Brother Benjamin the other day," the sister said. "He repaired the broken window in my room. I heard that you and your two friends are from Hungary."

"The Abbey of Archhalma. All three of us are from there."

Sister Hildegarde laughed.

"Why is that funny?" Brother Jacob asked, testing the zipper on one of the boots.

"I'm sorry to laugh, brother. But I believe the monastery is called the Archabbey of Pannonhalma. You can speak Hungarian to me. I'm fluent in it."

"Are you Hungarian?" the brother inquired.

"No, I'm an Austrian. I learned the language from some Hungarian sisters who once stayed at the monastery."

"How long have you been here?" Brother Jacob inquired.

"Seems like forever sometimes. Who are you making the boots for?"

Brother Jacob went silent for a moment, then he spurted a reply: "Abbot Zebedee."

"Oh . . . how nice of you. My winter boots need new soles. Could you fix them?"

"I'd be happy to."

"There's no hurry, brother. Winter won't be around for a few months." The sister warned in Hungarian, "Prior Mueller is suspicious of you, and Brother Benjamin—he'll want to ask you questions. He's not to be trusted."

The shoemaker looked up. "I don't understand. What are you talking about?"

Brother Jacob put the boot aside and reached for the other one.

"Oh, I think you do, brother. The abbot told me everything about you and your two friends. You've all come from Hungary, but not from the Archabbey of Pannonhalma. You and Brother Benjamin once lived in Beregszász. Brother Zohar is from Budapest. The three of you recently came from the camp in Mauthausen."

"How do you know all this?" the shoemaker inquired.

"Abbot Zebedee told me. There's no reason to lie, brother. And the boots you're making are not for the abbot. I highly doubt he'd wear Nazi boots. Besides . . . if they were for him, they'd be too small for his feet. Those look like a size ten. The abbot wears a size thirteen."

"What else did the abbot tell you?"

"We spoke about Major Himmel—the man who brought you from the camp. I know the major. And his wife. We come from the same place."

"Oh?"

"There's no need to be frightened, Mr. Katz. Your secrets are safe with me. I'll tell no one."

Brother Jacob nervously held up the boot and inspected it.

"You do superb work, brother."

"Thank you."

"I visited the camp a couple years ago," Sister Hildegard mentioned.

"Mauthausen?"

"*Igen*. Some of the sisters and I did charity work there. Horrible place. Hundreds die every day. May God have mercy on their souls. I'm here to help you and your two friends keep safe from the Nazis. You must be careful. Prior Mueller has a friend at the camp. They talk sometimes. His name is Sergeant Heimlich."

"We've met," Brother Katz mentioned. "Should I tell Brother Benjamin and Brother Zohar about this?"

"I already have. It's been nice chatting with you, brother. I'll bring you my boots tomorrow. Winter will be here before you know it."

22

Autumn arrived. And the leaves around Saint Clemens gradually changed to vibrant hues of cadmium orange, golden yellow, bright saffron, fiery red, burnt carmine, vermilion, primrose, livid pink, and then finally dead-leaf brown. In the last days of October strong winds and heavy rains came, and all the trees and bushes stood naked around the monastery. (All except for the evergreens that is.) The weather turned cool and dry; and for a week, the sisters and brothers raked the leaves into several large piles and burned the foliage under clear night skies. Sometimes, but not always, the fragrant, glowing red bonfires would completely cloak the odorous smoke that blew in from Mauthausen and its sub-camps.

By the beginning of November, the first frost collected on the lawns and gardens at the abbey. Preparing for winter, the rabbits, foxes, weasels, lynx, deer, and wolves took refuge deep within the evergreen forest, where they grew their warm winter coats. The creatures watched as the landscape surrounding the monastery turned barren and bleak. Little gray and brown field mice pitter-pattered outside the doors of Saint Clemens, hoping to gain access before the first snowfall.

* * *

On Ben's 25th birthday, the third week in November, after breakfast, he, Brother Zohar, and Brother Jacob put on their coats and gloves and gathered out in the chilly cloister.

They rested on a bench where Ben always sat, under a leafless birch tree. The late autumn sun weakly shone between the birch branches and alighted upon the saintly statues there. The blue birds which once nested in the trees had flown south and were replaced by two ominous-looking crows that sang a raspy operetta of caws, clicks and shrieks. To scare off the large black birds, Zohar stood like a tall scarecrow with his arms straight out. The lanky brother sat.

The two men listened while Ben finally divulged his secret. Of course, they were skeptical at first, when he told them what happened to him inside Sister Hildegard's room, the day he repaired her window. How he walked into the spicy-sweet frankincense-filled room, saw the mysterious amethyst light, and the manner in which he had left his physical body and viewed it from above. The men became excited when Ben spoke about Sister Hildegard; how she stood naked by the broken window, her broad, magnificent golden wings etched with white on their fringes; the mystical way in which she revealed herself, along with the divine nature of everything. The other two brothers believed him in the end.

Later that afternoon, after supper, Sister Hildegard surprised Brother Benjamin with a huge birthday cake she had decorated with a chocolate buttercream frosting. Abbot Zebedee, Prior Mueller, and all the brothers and sisters joyfully watched as Ben made a wish and blew out three candles on the cake. Everyone enjoyed a chocolaty slice, an extra glass of wine, and a healthy shot of Benedictine and Brandy.

That evening, the wind carried in a freeze from the Alps, and the brothers and sisters fired up the potbelly stoves and hearths inside the abbey. Billowy dark clouds formed, and large snowflakes splattered onto Abbot Zebedee's windowsill outside his office. He happily pondered the snow fall. The telephone rang. Commandant Graben greeted him on the other end. And they talked for a few minutes. Afterward, the abbot quickly left his office and rushed to Prior Mueller's room down the hall. He knocked.

"Who is it?" the prior asked as he was just about to blow out his oil-lamp and climb into bed.

"Abbot Zebedee."

"I'm going to sleep," he said behind the door. "Can it wait till tomorrow morning?"

"I'm afraid not."

The prior opened his door.

"What is it, Abbot?"

"My apologies for disturbing you so late. Abbot Joseph at Melk Abbey asked me a big favor. He needs someone to help him organize his books for a few days. His prior fell sick; he's in bed with pneumonia. I told him you would do it. I'm giving you some money to give him, since we're financially stable right now."

"When will all this be taking place?" Prior Mueller inquired.

"Tomorrow." The abbot handed the prior an envelope. "There's one thousand deutsche marks inside. Give it to Abbot Joseph when you arrive. Pack a bag now. You'll leave for Melk Abbey the first thing in the morning. A car will take you and bring you back. Sleep well, Prior. And God bless you for helping out."

"*Ja, gut nacht,* Abbot," he said in a coarse-grated German.

The abbot strode through the hall and walked his great body up the stairs to the monks' dormitory. He breathed heavily as he knocked on Brother Benjamin's door.

"Abbot Zebedee . . . what's the matter?"

"Something unexpected came up—we have to talk."

"Come in."

"I just got off the phone with the commandant at Mauthausen. He told me the Gestapo will visit the monastery two days from now."

"How would that concern me?" Ben inquired.

"The commandant doesn't know that you and your two friends are here."

"But I thought he and the major arranged all this," Ben said.

"Never mind. If the commandant finds out—we'll all be dead. I have to figure out what to do. It's cold in here," the abbot said, as he rubbed his large hands together.

"I'll build a fire."

Ben quickly crumpled up newspaper and put it inside the small wood-burning stove; he added kindling, struck a match, and the paper ignited. The monk inserted some split logs before closing the door on the stove.

"Napoleon Bonaparte once stayed in this room," the abbot mentioned.

"Oh?"

"When the French occupied Austria. Napoleon and his army traveled through this area. That's the rumor I heard anyway. I have a great idea, brother."

"What is it?" Ben asked while he opened the flue on the stove pipe, allowing the fire to cook hotter. In a few moments the room became toasty warm. Outside, the wind howled.

"Please, have a seat, Abbot."

"Danke."

Abbot Zebedee rested on the chair by the desk, crossing his brawny arms over his barrel chest. Ben sat on the bed and listened, while the abbot spoke to him in German.

23

Raphael removed a large cardboard box from the trunk of Major Himmel's Mercedes, and he leaned it against the car. The major buttoned his long wool coat, stepped from the car, and a thin layer of frozen snow crunched beneath his well-worn military boots. He stood at the entrance of Saint Clemens and read a notice on the door: Doorbell is broken. Please use the doorknocker. The sound of the knocker reverberated within the abbey's wide, cold hallway. The noise awakened a snowy owl outside, who had taken up residence inside the eaves of a cupola above. The white-feathered creature hooted once, closed its yellow eyes, and then buried its black beak inside the warmth of its chest feathers. The owl slept the entire day before its nightly hunt for dinner.

The major was about to knock again when a monk opened the front door.

"Good morning, Major. How can I help you?"

"Good morning, Brother Zebulon. I have a delivery for Abbot Zebedee."

By coincidence, the man of great stature happened to be close by, walking the abbey's Saint Bernard.

"Here he is now. He's just come back from his morning walk," the welcoming monk announced. "You have a visitor Abbot."

"Good morning, Abbot Zebedee."

"Major Himmel. What a pleasant surprise," the abbot said. "He's harmless."

The Saint Bernard approached the high-ranking officer and licked his glove-less hand. The major stroked the dog's big furry head.

"How are those three monks from Pannonhalma working out?" the major inquired.

"Excellent."

"Good. I'm here to pick up the boots I ordered from the shoemaker—so I thought I'd bring the monastery an early Christmas present. It's in the box by the car.

The major pointed to the large rectangular box that had a festive red bow and ribbon tied around it. FRAGILE GLASS was written on the front and back of the box.

"Oh, splendid," the abbot said.

"There are three stained-glass windows inside," the major announced. "To replace the broken ones in the chapel. It was quite drafty in there the last time my wife and I were here."

"How kind of you, Major." The abbot turned to a monk who was standing by the doorway. "Have Brother Benjamin come to the front entrance immediately. Inform him that a delivery of glass has just arrived. And tell him to bring the handcart with him."

"Where might the glazier be?" the monk asked.

"I believe he's working in the infirmary," the abbot replied. "Just curious, Major. How did you know the size of the glass?"

"I measured a frame the last time I was here," he replied. "I'm pretty handy with a ruler, you know. Oh, by the way, do you happen to know where Brother Zohar is working today? I would like a word with him after I collect my new boots."

"He's putting up Christmas lights in the dining room. Brother Zebulon will accompany you through the abbey. And Major?"

"*Ja?*"

"After you finish your business, you and your driver should come by my office later. I'll have some sandwiches and coffee prepared before you get back on the road."

"*Wunderbar.*"

* * *

Major Himmel and Brother Zebulon approached the shoemaker's workbench.

"Good morning, Brother Jacob."

"Ah, Major. It's nice to see you again. Your boots are ready. I was just putting a final polish on them."

"They look fabulous!" the major declared. "Don't they, Brother Zebulon?"

The elderly monk smiled and nodded his head in agreement. The major picked up a boot and felt the smooth leather. The mirror-like shine on the shoe enabled the major to see his true reflection.

"Try them on," Brother Jacob said.

"Before I forget . . . here's my payment for the boots. It's five hundred deutsche marks. That should be enough to cover the cost of your labor and materials."

"I can't accept that, Major. It's more money, I would charge to make ten pairs of boots."

"Take it," the major said, handing the shoemaker an envelope. "You'll need the money after you leave the monastery."

"*Danke Schön,* Major."

"*Bitte schön.*"

The shoemaker stashed the money in his robe pocket. The major sat on a chair, and Brother Jacob helped him remove his old boots. The brother helped the officer put his feet inside the new pair of boots and zipped them up.

"Take a walk and see how they feel."

The major stood and walked around some.

What do you think, Major?"

He looked at the shoemaker and broadly smiled.

"They're very comfortable. You did a wonderful job, brother. I'll be sure to recommend you to my higher-ups."

"Wear them in good health, Major."

"*Danke schön.* You can burn the old boots," the major instructed. He turned to Brother Zebulon. "Shall we see the electrician now?"

24

At eight o'clock in the morning, a colorless sun broke through a dark haze above Mauthausen, while a *Kübelwagen* and two military trucks exited the camp, turning a light cover of snow into slush along the slippery route. A zealous Sergeant Heimlich had detached a Nazi convoy which consisted of himself, Corporal Wagner, three German shepherds, and eight other gun-toting Gestapo. The convoy slowly drove up a treacherously steep hill before sledding into Saint Clemens's snow-covered parking lot. The warmly dressed militia got out of their vehicles and tiredly flapped their arms up and down and goose-stepped past the bell tower.

Long pointed icicles had formed under the parapets above the entrance; one broke loose and dropped, barely missing the sergeant's head as he overanxiously used the doorknocker several times. Abbot Zebedee finally appeared.

"Good morning, Sergeant Heimlich. Haven't seen you in ages."

"*Ja—guten morgen*, Abbot. It's time you fixed your doorbell. *Hei?*"

"Our electrician will see to it soon, Sergeant. Come in, gentlemen. And please wipe the snow off your boots. I have hot refreshments prepared for you in the dining hall. Right this way."

The Gestapo marched inside and slowly lumbered through the hall. A large group of hooded nuns nervously passed and rapidly vanished down the marble-floored corridor. The militia was escorted into the dining hall and seated at a long table, where brothers and sisters served them a continental breakfast of coffee, tea, and warmed-up apple strudel.

"How's life back at Mauthausen, Sergeant?" Abbot Zebedee asked while a sister poured steaming hot coffee into the Nazi's cup.

The sergeant gobbled down a bite of strudel and replied, "*Alles ist gut.* We're liquidating more and more Jews every day. In addition to any gentile political dissidents who are uncooperative with the Führer's cause."

"And this is what he calls the final solution?" the abbot inquired.

"That's correct."

"May the good Lord have mercy on their souls," the abbot said, making the sign of the cross.

The sergeant brushed some strudel crumbs off his army coat and gave the large clergyman a look of disapproval.

"You know, Abbot. Speaking in such a manner could be considered quite dangerous for you. It's forbidden to sympathize with the enemy. I could easily arrange a private cell for you in Mauthausen."

The abbot remained sullen faced.

"Do you understand me, Abbot?"

"Yes, of course."

"Good. Who made the apple strudel?" the sergeant asked, reaching for another pastry.

"A sister here bakes it."

"It's delicious. Could you get me the recipe?" the sergeant inquired.

"I'll see about it."

"And Commandant Graben wants more bottles of wine and brandy. All our supplies are waning. Winter has arrived early this year. We'll need blankets, socks, and whatever food provisions you can provide us."

"Don't worry, Sergeant. It'll all be prepared before you leave."

"*Gut.* And where are the brothers and sisters right now? It's quiet as a church mouse in here."

"You're in a monastery, Sergeant ... don't forget. Many of the brothers and sisters are praying in the chapel right now. The rest are busy with their various chores throughout the abbey."

"I see."

The other men in the Gestapo made idle conversation while they chain-smoked bad-smelling cigarettes, polluting the atmosphere inside the dining hall. Abbot Zebedee asked a monk to open one of the windows there. A freezing fresh air blew in.

"And where's my good friend, Prior Mueller?" the blue-eyed sergeant asked the abbot.

"He took a few days leave at Melk Abbey."

"That's a shame; I was hoping to speak with him," the Nazi said. "Have you heard about the escape that occurred at the camp not long ago?"

"No, Sergeant. I haven't. We lead a fairly reclusive life at Saint Clemens. I wasn't aware of an escape."

"It was announced over the radio. I'm sure you must have a radio."

"We do. But I seldom have time to listen to current events."

"You should. We're still looking for a handful of escaped prisoners who might have wandered through this area. Three Hungarian men in particular. You haven't seen them at the monastery by any chance?"

"I doubt anyone besides a monk, or a sister could survive this place for very long," the abbot replied. "What do these Hungarian men look like, Sergeant?"

"One has straight black hair, is young, tall, and skinny. Olive-colored complexion. He's a Christian man, and an electrician. Another man is a light-skinned Jew in his early twenties. He's short, has brown hair, hazel green eyes, and quite muscular. He's got a birthmark on the side of one of his nostrils. Works with glass. The other escapee is a Jew also. Mid-forties I would say. He's a short and scrawny looking fellow. Light-skinned as well. He's a shoemaker."

"Do any of these Hungarian men wear eyeglasses by any chance?" the abbot questioned.

"*Nein.*"

"You and your men are welcome to look around—but I doubt it will be much use," the abbot said.

"Just the same, we'll require a complete search inside and outside the monastery. And while we're occupied with that, prepare the supplies I requested. And don't forget about that delicious Benedictine and Brandy you make here. *Achtung!* Wagner?"

"*Ja*, Sergeant?"

"The abbot will be accompanying you to the kitchen and bakery now. Afterward, he'll take you up to the library. You three men search the chapel, the offices, the laundry, the basement, the catacombs, and outside around the building. Take the dogs with you. The other five men and I will check the brothers' and sisters' rooms. Let's go."

* * *

In the busy kitchen of the monastery, Corporal Wagner occasionally saw double when he removed his coke-bottle eyeglasses and wiped the vapor off them with a cloth; he returned them to his squinch-eyed face then observed the brothers and sisters chop vegetables and scale, clean, and bone fresh fish that was caught in the Danube. Other nuns and monks scrubbed everything from top to bottom while the near-sighted Nazi inspected the immaculate kitchen. The corporal approached a stove where a short but able-bodied sister stood. The bangs of a blonde wig concealed her forehead while a heavy make-up had been applied to her cheeks, nose, and chin. Eyeglasses framed her face. The contents in the pot she was stirring gave off a steamy pungent odor of onion, oregano, black pepper, garlic, and cabbage. The sister glanced up at the Nazi through her steamed-up spectacles. He sneezed.

"Something smells *wunderbar*," the corporal said. "What's for supper, *fräulein*?"

The broad-bodied sister leaned over the pot while marinating its contents. She replied in a high-pitched German, "Stuffed cabbage. *Heil Hellmenz* Capitan."

"Hungarian food. It smells delicious, sister. Carry on with your work. And *heil Hellmenz*."

The strong nun covered the pot of stuffed cabbage, and she bent down and whispered in the ear of a tall sister who was scrubbing the floor on her hands and knees. That sister also wore eyeglasses. "We're dead meat if they find the commandant's radio in your room," Brother Benjamin softly spoke.

"It's gone," Brother Zohar whispered back. "Major Himmel took it from me yesterday."

* * *

Two men from the Gestapo patiently waited in the monastery's cold and dimly lit wine cellar while an older nun packed bottles of wine and liquor into boxes. The hooded sister was short and wore horn-rimmed glasses. The soldiers carried out the boxes and loaded them onto the back of a truck. One of them mentioned to the other while they took a cigarette break outside, "Manfred. Did you see how ugly that sister looked down there?"

"Ja. She looks like my grandmother. C'mon, Werner—we have more boxes to load—this place gives me the creeps already."

"Her perfume smelled nice, Manfred."

"*Schnell,* Werner."

Disguised in a Benedictine nun's habit, makeup, pretty red lipstick, and the horn-rimmed eyeglasses: Brother Jacob wiped the bottles in a dark alcove of the wine cellar, while the two soldiers left with the last boxes of *vino* and dark beer.

In the bakery, Sister Hildegard gathered up a large pile of bread dough from the mixer, and she kneaded it on a floured worktable. The sister looked up when the abbot and the corporal entered the bakery. She nodded and gave the Nazi a teeth-clenched smile.

"Corporal, this is our hard-working headbaker, Sister Hildegard," the abbot introduced. "Corporal Wagner is here with the Gestapo, Sister. They're looking for some prisoners who've escaped from Mauthausen."

"Oh?"

"*Igen.*"

The sister smiled and sprinkled some bread flour onto her worktable.

"Be my guest," she said, forming the soft dough into a ball, and placing it onto a parchment-covered bake pan to proof. She held another clump of dough and started working with that.

"By the way, Sister, do you happen to have the recipe for your apple strudel? Sergeant Heimlich would like to borrow it," the abbot said.

"It's in my drawer. I'll get it for you."

While the corporal slid his dirty fingernails along the baker's workbench, he sniffed the doughy air and stuck two of his fingers into a bowl of whipped cream. He licked his fingers then smiled. The abbot showed him through the rest of the bakeshop, and the two men turned to leave.

"I found the recipe, Abbot," the sister said. She handed him an index card.

"Thank you, sister. Have a blessed day."

"You as well, gentlemen."

After the men left, Sister Hildegard dumped the bowl of whipped cream down the sink.

The abbot and the corporal proceeded to the library.

* * *

"Watch your step, Corporal," the abbot warned. "You're not afraid of heights, are you? It's a bit of a climb."

"Nein."

The two men slowly ascended the steep spiral staircase. The low-ranking Nazi soldier nervously held onto the wrought-iron railing and glanced at the colorful frescoes painted high above his head. They finally reached the top step and entered a large room filled with sunlight.

"This is our library. Do you like to read, Corporal?" the abbot asked.

"It's not one of my favorite pastimes."

The circular ascent had caused the corporal's focus to spin around and make his head swim momentarily.

"Are you all right, C*apitan*?"

"*Ja,*" the corporal replied as he wiped the sweat from his brow, regained his equilibrium, and then followed the abbot through the library.

"This is our head librarian, Brother Martin," the abbot introduced. "Brother Martin, meet Corporal Wagner. He's from the camp at Mauthausen. I'll be giving him a tour of the library."

"Welcome, Corporal," the librarian spoke as he made the sign of the cross before returning his attention to the Book of Proverbs.

"*Danke.*"

"This way," the abbot said. "Our library houses some of the oldest religious manuscripts in the world, but that wouldn't interest you much. Not being a reader."

"*Nein.*"

After the abbot and the corporal were finished, they approached the librarian's desk again.

"Well, I hope that satisfies your curiosity, Corporal Wagner," Brother Martin said. "You can rest assured . . . we're not hiding any of your escaped prisoners up here."

"*Gut,*" the corporal said.

He and the abbot left for the long staircase again.

"Watch your step," Abbot Zebedee said while he motioned for the soldier to go first.

After a few turns around the spiral stairs, Corporal Wagner stopped to clean his fogged-up glasses, when they slipped from his hands. He tried to catch them, but he lost his balance and fell over the railing and plummeted to the bottom. A sister who witnessed the fall heard the corporal's neck crack when he hit the hard marble floor. Her loud shrieks echoed through the monastery.

The librarian jumped off his stool and ran to the top of the staircase. "Oh, Jesus!"

Shocked, the abbot looked over the railing. "Hurry. Someone notify the ambulance!" he hollered in vain.

Miraculously, the corporal's thick glass lenses remained intact when they bounced off the stairs and landed on the floor. Several brothers and sisters gathered around the corporal while he convulsed some, then went still. The abbot reached the bottom of the staircase and quickly approached the group.

"Call the doctor," he ordered.

Feeling the corporal's pulse, a monk answered, "That won't be necessary, Abbot; he's already gone."

"Oh, my God," the abbot said, as he bowed his head and made the sign of the cross.

Sergeant Heimlich and a few of the other Nazis came running after they heard the commotion.

"What happened to him?" the sergeant asked.

"He fell off the stairs," the abbot replied, pointing to the top of the staircase. "He was rushing and lost his balance—it was an accident."

"An accident?" the sergeant questioned as he closed the dead man's eyes.

"Yes," the abbot explained, "he dropped his glasses and fell over the railing when he tried to catch them."

"Perhaps you accidentally pushed him, *hei*, Abbot?"

"Definitely not—he was too far ahead of me."

"Put him on the truck," the sergeant ordered two of the monks. "Are all our supplies packed?" he asked one of the men from the Gestapo.

"*Ja.*"

"Let's get out of here, then," the sergeant gruffly said. "And you're coming with us, Abbot."

"Why on earth for?"

"I believe the commandant will need to interrogate you about the corporal's death."

"But I had nothing to do with it," he pleaded.

"Then you'll explain that to the commandant. Along with how sympathetic you feel about the Jews."

"I'll need to get my hat and coat first."

"Hurry, then."

* * *

The next day, Prior Mueller returned to Saint Clemens and found that Abbot Zebedee was absent from his post. He read a note taped to his desk, informing him about the mishap which took place at the monastery, and that the abbot had been taken to the concentration camp for interrogation. The message had been signed by Prioress Sister Saint Andrews. The prior picked up the telephone and nervously dialed the camp. A switchboard operator answered:

"Good morning. Mauthausen concentration camp, can I help you?"

"Hello. Could you please connect me with the commandant," the prior asked.

"Just a moment, please."

While the prior waited to be connected, he noticed a pair of coke-bottle eyeglasses on Abbot Zebedee's desk. He looked out the window at the wind-swirling snow. A white-tailed rabbit ran past.

"Commandant Graben speaking."

"Hello, Commandant. This is Prior Mueller from Saint Clemens Monastery."

"Morning, Prior, I was expecting a call from you."

"When will Abbot Zebedee be returning to Saint Clemens?" the prior inquired.

"I have some good news and bad news for you, Mr. Mueller. Unfortunately—because of the terrible incident that happened at the monastery—the abbot won't be coming back to the monastery any time soon."

"Why is that?"

"From the information we gathered during our interrogation with Abbot Zebedee, a tribunal charged him with one count of manslaughter and two counts of verbally sympathizing with the enemy. It's very unfortunate, but he was sentenced to ten years imprisonment with hard labor. The good news is you'll be taking over the abbot's position immediately. Have a nice day. Abbot Mueller."

25

December 25, 1944

After everyone at the monastery ate their Christmas dinner of Weiner Schnitzel, yams, green peas, and Linzer Torte, Abbot Mueller and Brother Martin celebrated the rest of the holiday by breaking into the last two bottles of Abbot Zebedee's private stock of Chianti. The two men became increasingly intoxicated while they listened to a BBC broadcast on the latest developments of World War II:

"On Christmas day, the American Third Army, under the leadership of General George Patton, the Second US Armored Division, halted enemy tanks short of the Meuse River," a radio announcer spoke.

"It sounds like the Germans may be retreating," Brother Martin said while Abbot Mueller poured more red wine into their glasses.

"That's a shame," the abbot remarked.

By the 16th of January 1945, the German army would ultimately lose the Battle of the Bulge, which was fought in the Ardennes Forest of Belgium and Luxembourg. On January 27, 1945, Soviet troops liberated the Auschwitz concentration camp, marking the beginning of the end of the Holocaust.

* * *

In the dead of winter, Brother Benjamin put on his wool coat and went outside to the woodshed. A diamond night sky sparkled above. An icy air embraced the monk's neck. He shivered. The mercury was below zero. He grasped a long-handled ax and proceeded to split a pile of birch and maple logs. After twenty minutes of hard physical exertion, Ben leaned the ax inside the woodshed and loaded the split wood into a wheelbarrow. He wiped his forehead then steered the wheelbarrow through a back entrance, carting the wood inside the chapel. He removed his coat, gloves and scarf and started stacking the split wood beside a hearth. He fed the fire, rested on a pew, and admired the three stained-glass windows he had installed a month ago. The hearth's blazing orange flames magically reflected off the frost-covered glass.

April 1945

As he cleaned up his work area in the basement, Brother Benjamin heard thawing sheets of ice and snow slide off the monastery roof and crash to the ground. The snowy owl that had wintered on the cupola was awakened by the noise, and it flew off toward some tall spruce trees. It never returned. Ben felt the monastery wasn't quite the same without Abbot Zebedee. He placed a broom and dustpan aside, put on his coat, and took a long walk around the grounds. He rubbed the sun's heat into his arms, breathed the fresh country air, and then moved at a slightly faster pace. The ice on the

Danube had melted, and the spring sunlight gave life to the tiny greenish buds on the trees and bushes. *The leaves will appear again soon,* he thought. Before continuing his hike, Brother Benjamin stopped to watch a long black barge drift with the river's current; he recognized the boat's white granite cargo.

* * *

Well into April, Brother Benjamin spent more time outdoors. He had repaired most of the broken windows in the abbey, so he assisted some other brothers and sisters till the gardens and prepare the soil for the first planting of vegetable seedlings that had been started in the monastery's greenhouse.

* * *

In the basement of the Saint Clemens, Brother Jacob continued to work on the sisters' and brothers' shoes. He often ruminated about his wife, occasionally shedding tears over the happier times they had spent in Beregszász.

* * *

Brother Zohar occupied himself with his electrical duties throughout the abbey. He finally addressed the broken doorbell at the front entrance. He installed a new bell and tested it by pressing his lanky finger on the round button. It worked. He rang the bell a couple more times before an irate Abbot Mueller approached him in the vestibule.

"Brother Zohar. What is going on with that blessed bell? I thought you fixed it."

Zohar gave the abbot a broad smile. "I have. It's working now," the electrician happily replied.

"I heard! Now take down those Christmas lights around the monastery. It's almost the end of April."

Brother Zohar tapped his heels together and raised his arm in a German military salute. *"Jawohl, Capitan."*

* * *

When the month of May arrived, Sister Hildegard would finish her early morning tasks in the bakery and go outside to help Sister Saint Andrews plant tulip bulbs in the garden facing the abbot's office window. They would laugh the whole time, while the baker's long blond hair flew in the blustery wind. Her lips usually painted a rich, pomegranate red. Abbot Mueller would scornfully watch the two women through his window.

* * *

Three weeks went by, and the flower bulbs the two sisters had planted vigorously sprouted. A length of time afterward, several crimson, white, yellow, and pink paper-thin tulips bloomed in the garden. On a sunny afternoon, Sister Hildegard cut a wicker basketful of the flowers, left the garden, and carried it into the hallway of the abbey. She stopped to rest near Abbot Mueller's office, and, by coincidence, she clearly heard him having a conversation on the telephone.

"Sergeant, I believe there's something *rotten in Denmark* at the monastery," the abbot announced.

"What do you mean?"

"Haven't you heard of that expression before?" the abbot asked.

"Of course, I have. Get to the fucking point, Mueller."

"A sister who works in the laundry here found something inside the pocket of a monk's robe."

"What is it?"

"A faded yellow document of some sort. It looks official. I have it in front of me right now," the abbot replied.

"Oh?"

"It's been washed out several times," the abbot stated. "Let me look at it with a magnifying glass. Ah, that's a little clearer, but the writing is too faded. There appears to be a signature. And some kind of symbol. I can't decipher it."

"The commandant needs more wine," the sergeant said. "I'll be at the monastery in the morning to look at it. *Gut nacht,* Abbot."

"I look forward to seeing you, Sergeant. *Gut nacht.*"

Abbot Mueller hung up the phone and set the faded yellow document aside, while Sister Hildegard's shadow swiftly passed his open doorway. She hastened toward the dining hall and placed the basket of flowers onto a table.

26

Sister Hildegard unexpectedly appeared at Ben's worktable while he steadily guided his glass cutter along a windowpane. He looked up startled and misdirected the line of the glass cutter, leaving the pane unusable. He discarded the glass waste into a metal barrel.

"Sister Hildegard—I'm surprised to see you here this hour—thought you'd be getting ready for supper."

"Greetings, Brother Benjamin. You and your two friends must leave the monastery tonight."

"Why?"

"We can't talk here—come with me—we'll go out to the cloister."

Ben darkened the light above his table, and they went outside and walked to a far end of the quadrangle, where the full moon's dazzling pearl-white glow caused a group of stone saints there to look alive. The sister peeked from behind a statue, taking care nobody else was around to listen.

"You and the other two brothers are no longer safe here. I overheard Abbot Mueller talk on the phone with his friend from Mauthausen. Sergeant Heimlich. He said a sister who works in the laundry found a suspicious-looking document in the pocket of a monk's robe. It may have come from the concentration camp. Mueller got a hold of it—and informed the sergeant. One of you must have accidentally placed it in the robe when you changed clothes. The Gestapo are coming here early tomorrow morning. You'll have to leave tonight."

"How?" Ben asked.

"I'll steal the keys to the monastery's car and drive you across the border into Switzerland. Once you get there, you'll be out of harm's way."

"None of us have passports."

"You don't need them. You'll apply for political asylum at the border."

"What about Abbot Mueller?" Ben asked. "I would think he'd be suspicious of the slightest activity around here."

"I'll take care of him," the sister said, "just tell the other brothers to prepare to leave tonight. And don't speak about this at the supper table. I don't want you to draw any unnecessary attention. Someone's coming—quick—we'll leave through the garden."

* * *

Sister Hildegard rushed to the apothecary's office, picked the door lock, and then broke the glass on a medicine cabinet. She discovered a bottle of sleeping pills, turned off the light, and then flew down the hall to the bakery. She removed a gold heart locket from around her neck and pulled a latch to open the little locket door. She ground the white pills in a mortar and pestle before filling the locket with the powdered sedative.

* * *

Abbot Mueller had entered the dining hall and noticed the neglected basket of fresh-cut tulips. He questioned a youthful sister who was setting a dinner table.

"Sister Mary?"

"Yes, Abbot?"

"What are these damn flowers doing here?"

"I don't know."

"Get them in water before supper starts."

"Yes, Abbot, I'll do it right away."

"And fetch me a bottle of red wine. A cabernet preferably."

"Yes, sir."

The young sister brought the basket of tulips to the kitchen, and she selected a bottle of cabernet from a wine rack.

"I'll get the abbot his wine, Sister Mary," Sister Hildegard said. "You attend to the flowers now. Please."

"Yes, Sister."

Sister Mary placed the tulips into three vases and added water from the sink. She brought the vases to the dining hall and proceeded to set them on two long tables.

"Where's that bottle of wine, sister?"

"Sister Hildegard is seeing to it," Sister Mary replied.

"*Gut,*" the abbot said while ogling the young nun's softly curved figure.

Meanwhile, Sister Hildegard carried a wine bottle to the back storeroom and opened it with a corkscrew. She discreetly added the white powder from her heart locket, reinserted the cork, shook the bottle, and then delivered it to Abbot Mueller. She removed the cork and poured him a glass. He smiled and thanked her.

In the meantime, monks and nuns carried baskets of bread and butter out to the dining hall while the kitchen staff brought out supper. Soon afterward, the dining hall filled with brothers and sisters. The monks sat and held hands at their long table; the sisters held hands at theirs. They said grace before helping themselves to steaming-hot stuffed cabbage. Ben's mother's recipe.

When he was almost through eating supper, Abbot Mueller noticed that the sisters' and brothers' faces had become animated and distorted. He finished his second glass of wine, and everyone's voice sounded weird and garbled. The abbot started laughing for no reason. The drug inside the wine had taken effect. He swirled around the alcohol, spilling some onto the skirt of his robe. He inhaled the fruity bouquet while briefly noticing a powdery white substance on the surface. The abbot guzzled the wine and poured himself another glass. With his senses greatly impaired, he loudly called to the young sister who he had spoken to earlier. She was sweeping the floor nearby.

"Sister Mary."

"Yes, Abbot?"

"Come over here, please."

She stopped sweeping and approached him. "Do you need something, Abbot?"

He suddenly grabbed her wrist, twirled her around and firmly slapped her behind. "What room number are you in, Sister? I'd like to have sex with you tonight."

"Abbot—please!" Sister Mary declared as she pulled herself away from him and left.

The abbot laughed boisterously and banged his fists on the table. His drunken face twisted while the room spun in a wobbly circle. The brothers and sisters filed out of the dining hall, except for Sister Hildegard and Brothers Ben, Jacob, and Zohar. The abbot knocked over his wine glass and it shattered on the floor.

"It's time for bed, Abbot," Sister Hildegard told him. "Let's take him to his room."

The brothers helped the abbot stand, and they assisted him back to his room on the first floor. They stood in front of his locked door.

"Quick—someone reach into his pocket—and grab his keys," the sister instructed.

Ben fished out the abbot's keys and gave them to the sister. She unlocked the door, and they put the sedated man to bed. Brother Jacob removed the abbot's shoes while Ben gently set his head on a pillow. Sister Hildegard covered the snoring abbot with a blanket. Zohar darkened the oil lamp, and they left the room and scurried down the hallway.

27

While Sister Hildegard and the three brothers searched for the keys to the monastery's blue Benz, Ben scattered papers on the abbot's desk and completely overlooked his former work pass at Mauthausen.

"I can't find them," the sister said. "He usually hangs them on this hook."

Zohar moved a bottle that sat on a shelf. Behind it, laid a set of car keys. He dangled them in the air, "Is this what we're looking for?"

"Yes," the sister replied, and the lanky man tossed them to her. "Let's go, brothers—quickly."

They left the office, bolted down the hallway and out the front entrance. They got into a blue Mercedes. Ben sat in the front passenger seat while the other two got in the back. The sister nervously placed the keys into the ignition. The engine wouldn't start at first. She pumped the gas pedal and turned the key again. That time it worked. She revved the motor. Soon after, hard pellets of rain hammered the windshield. It thundered, and lightning struck the crosses on the monastery roof. The sister turned the wipers on high while Sister Saint Andrews pulled aside a curtain and observed them from a second-floor window. Sister Hildegarde burnt rubber as she tore out of the parking lot and drove down the steep driveway. They sped past the village of Melk and headed toward the Autobahn.

* * *

After travelling a few kilometers, Ben broke the silence by asking Sister Hildegard.

"How far is to Switzerland?"

"About seven hours. Hope we have enough petrol to make it there."

"How much do we have?" Zohar inquired.

"Almost a full tank."

Just then, two German military vehicles passed the monastery's blue Mercedes from the opposite direction. The swastika flags on the outside of their vehicles rapidly flapped in the air.

"Oh, Christ!" Sister Hildegard exclaimed.

Brother Jacob glanced through the rear windshield. "Gestapo?" he asked.

"I'm afraid so," the sister replied. "They're probably on their way to the monastery. Hold on, brothers; the road's a little rough through here."

The sister peeled around a tight curve; the high beams startled two wild boars who were digging tubers on the roadside; the bristle-haired animals scampered into the woods.

The sister pulled onto the ramp to the Autobahn, accelerated, and then drove at a high rate of speed.

* * *

The drivers of two German military vehicles raced up a hill and slammed on their brakes at the front of the monastery. Looking bloodshot eyed through the late evening mist, Sergeant Heimlich and three other Nazis hammered their hard heels to the front door. The sergeant impatiently rang the doorbell until an elderly monk's face appeared from a small window-like opening on the door.

"A blessed night, isn't it, Officer?" Brother Zebulon greeted. "We needed the rain."

"Fuck you! Where is Abbot Mueller?" the sergeant inquired.

"He's fast asleep. It's late."

"Let us in. I'll wake him up. I have reason to believe some escaped prisoners from Mauthausen are hiding in the abbey."

"Oh, Lord Jesus," the monk said. He closed the small window, unlocked the door, and opened it for the Gestapo. They barged in, almost knocking the short monk to the floor.

"Take us to the abbot's room," the sergeant ordered as he tugged on the sleeve of the monk's robe.

"This way."

They walked down the hall, and the monk stopped by a door and pointed his trembling finger. "That's the abbot's room there."

The Nazis burst into the unlocked room and found the abbot dead asleep.

"Mueller, wake up!" the sergeant yelled.

He didn't stir. Sergeant Heimlich picked up a wash basin of cold water and threw it onto the abbot's face. His nailed-shut eyes popped open and dilated.

"What in God's name is going on here?" he inquired. "Sergeant—you're early. I thought you were coming in the morning."

"Get up!"

"It feels like I've been drugged," the abbot said, while he wrenched himself out of bed and put on his shoes. "My keys are missing. I probably left them in my office."

"Move!"

They briskly marched down to the abbot's office, where they found his keys in the lock of the open door. The lights burned within. The abbot's desk was in a disarray.

"Mother of God! Someone was in here," Abbot Mueller exclaimed, as he noticed the disturbed condition of the room.

Just then, Sister Saint Andrews approached the open doorway.

"Abbot, I saw Sister Hildegard drive away in the monastery car," she announced. "What in heaven's name are these soldiers doing here this hour?"

"When was that?" the sergeant asked the prioress.

"About forty minutes ago. I overheard her say she was going to drive to the border in Zurich."

"What!" the abbot shouted.

"That must have been the blue Mercedes we passed on the way here," one of the other Nazis mentioned.

"*Ja—*"

Abbot Mueller picked up the washed-out yellow document on his desk. "This is what I was telling you about on the telephone," he said as he handed it to the sergeant.

Sergeant Heimlich could barely recognize the stamped seal of Mauthausen, a black eagle and swastika underneath; his slap-dash signature; and Ben's printed but faded last name; Weiss, was somewhat legible.

"Weiss? You bastard," the sergeant said. "That's one of our work passes we use at the camp."

Sister Saint Andrews and Brother Zebulon covered their mouths.

"You have a monk at the monastery who knows how to cut glass and fix broken windows?" the sergeant inquired.

"*Ja*, a short, muscular-looking fellow. Brother Benjamin is his name. Why?"

"He's a Jew!" the sergeant screamed loud this time. "That was his work pass at Mauthausen. He escaped with a shoemaker and an electrician. Have they been here also?"

"For several months now," the sandy-eyed abbot replied. "Abbot Zebedee told me the three brothers came from a monastery in Hungary. The Archabbey of Pannonhalma."

"He lied to you. He was protecting the prisoners."

"I knew something was fishy from the start," Abbot Mueller stated.

"Crazy fool. Let's get out of here and find that Mercedes. There's only one road to Zurich from here," the sergeant told the other Gestapo.

28

A family of deer meandered across the Autobahn, approaching the shelter of their woodland home. Taking up the rear of the herd, the mother, a speckle-tailed doe, innocently clip-clopped to the middle of the highway, where it kicked over a small wooden box; the mother deer froze, heard a distinctive clicking noise, and then pensively watched her family safely enter the dark forest. Moments later, the speckle-tailed doe moved her hoof slightly, and a landmine exploded. It scattered chunks of asphalt and smoke high above the road. The blast threw the doe off her feet, and she landed on the roadside. Her hind leg had been severed while the other back limb dangled from bleeding tendons and fascia.

Sister Hildegard and the three brothers had heard the explosion while they neared the scene of the accident. The sister swerved around a crater in the road then stopped on the shoulder. From the cars headlights and burning brush, the sister and brothers observed the injured animal; its life-fluid rapidly poured from its arteries and veins.

"My God!" the sister declared. "Please help that poor creature. Hurry, Ben, open the glove compartment and take out the pistol. Be careful—it's loaded."

"Here. What's this for?" Ben asked while he cautiously handed the gun to the sister.

"I have to put the animal out of its misery."

"Oh."

The sister and the three men got out of the car and went over to where the speckle-tailed doe laid. It breathed heavily. The other deer had stopped soon after the explosion. By instinct, the herd must have sensed that a member of their clan, their mother, had fallen behind. The animals in the forest turned toward the road and listened while Sister Hildegard knelt and comforted the bleeding doe. The three brothers watched as the sister gently stroked the soft gray fur on its neck. The doe calmed a little, looking at everyone with her coffee-brown eyes. Then. The sister's glowing gold angel's wings appeared, and she spread them over the animal. The three brothers felt a powerful sensation in the air.

"What happened to me?" the speckle-tailed doe inquired.

"You must have stepped on a landmine," the angel replied. "It was an accident."

"My pain is excruciating."

"I know. Fear not, though, my lovely creature You'll be with the Almighty soon," the angelic being said."

The animal glanced above. "Your wings are beautiful. Are you an eagle?"

"No, I'm an angel. I've come to help you return home."

The brothers were awestruck as they watched the mother deer shed tears. In the forest, her family cried also.

"Is there a way this can be made better?" the doe beseeched the angel.

"Yes, there is."

Sister Hildegard made the sign of the cross, unlatched the safety on the pistol and placed the barrel against the doe's thumping heart. She pulled the trigger.

The men flinched.

"Let's go, brothers."

* * *

Farther down the Autobahn, Sister Hildegard drove by a troop of camp guards who were leading hundreds of bone-thin prisoners on a death-march along the roadside. They'd been taken out of Mauthausen's main and sub-camps, so the Nazis could avoid the approaching allied armies. Many of the prisoners on the march dropped dead from hunger, dehydration, sickness, and exhaustion. If anyone lagged behind, he or she had a bullet put in their head. The blue Mercedes shot past the throng of ragged specters, kapos and Nazi guards.

* * *

A couple hours later the sister drove into a tunnel; a freight train rolled by on the rails above. Its blaring horn echoed inside the hollow thoroughfare, as the sound of German police sirens wailed farther behind. The blue Mercedes Benz emerged from the tunnel, and a hint of daylight appeared.

"There's a sign up ahead," Zohar said. "It's two kilometers to Zurich."

Ben turned on the radio and tuned in an English-speaking station. A newscaster announced, "This is the latest news bulletin from the BBC in London. Today, the 8th of May 1945, Germany has officially surrendered. I repeat. German forces have surrendered. The war is over in Europe."

"Oh, thank God!" Sister Hildegard declared.

Everyone in the car was overjoyed as a spark of sunlight came over the trees. They watched while a buzz of military vehicles passed from the opposite direction. Soldiers happily waved while British, American, French, and Canadian flags triumphantly flew from their vehicles.

The blue Mercedes drew nearer to the Swiss border, when the German police vehicles caught up with them. Sister Hildegard glanced in the rearview mirror and saw the flashing red lights.

"We have them now," Sergeant Heimlich boasted, confidently gripping his silver Luger pistol. One of the

Gestapo opened a window of one of the *Kübelwagen,* and he yelled into a megaphone, "Pull the car over or we will shoot! Pull over. *Schnell!*"

A patch of dense fog suddenly descended upon the road, enveloping the Gestapo's vehicles and the blue Mercedes. When the thick gray mist lifted, Sergeant Heimlich and the other soldiers observed the blue Mercedes idling on the shoulder of the highway; the morning sun now shined brightly on its indigo hood. The *Kübelwagens* braked behind, and the Gestapo got out; they drew their weapons and surrounded the blue car. Someone rolled down the window on the passenger side of the Mercedes, and the sergeant stared in disbelief.

"Major Himmel! —What on earth are you doing here?"

"Hello, Sergeant."

"*Heil Hellmenz,*" the sergeant said, saluting with his arm high in the air. "We'll relieve you of the escaped prisoners now, Major."

"I think you made a big mistake, Sergeant," the major said. "And please. Lower your arm. Your armpit stinks."

"Where are the three escaped prisoners, Major?" the sergeant inquired while peering through the back window of the car.

"Are you out of your mind? —We have no prisoners with us."

The rear window opened, and Lieutenant Flügel and Captain Segan nodded from the back seat. "Lower your guns, gentlemen," the Lieutenant ordered. "The war is over, Sergeant. Germany surrendered less than twenty minutes ago. I'm sure you heard it on the radio."

"*Nein*," he replied, with an extremely puzzled look. The Gestapo holstered their pistols.

"Now, if you don't mind, gentlemen. We'll be continuing our journey into Switzerland," the major said. "We're meeting our wives at a lovely resort high in the Alps. Drive on, Raphael."

The three high-ranking officers smiled, rolled up their windows, and the gleaming blue Mercedes disappeared within the golden dawn.

* * *

Still attired in their robes from the monastery, Ben, Zohar, and Mr. Katz sat inside a room at a border station in Zurich. A Swiss woman dressed in a khaki uniform came out and served them egg sandwiches and coffee. They heard a train whistle not far-off.

"Now that the war is over—what are we going to do next?" Mr. Katz asked.

"You have money," Ben answered. "I suppose we could buy train tickets and return home to Beregszász."

"*Igen*. Maybe some of our friends and family will be there," Mr. Katz said. "And Zohar can go home to Budapest. And see his."

Tears fell from Zohar's eyes, "I have no friends or family left in Budapest. My mother and father died when I was only a child. My grandparents raised me. And I have no sisters or brothers. Nor aunts, uncles, or cousins that I know of. Perhaps, I could come with you guys?"

Ben consoled Zohar by placing his hand on the lanky man's shoulder.

"Of course, you can come with us, brother. We are your family now."

"Thank you, Ben."

"We'll build a new life for ourselves," Mr. Katz said. "If not in Beregszász then somewhere else."

"Perhaps we can go to America," Zohar optimistically mentioned, beaming a broad smile now. "I hear the streets there are paved with gold."

"*Igen*," Ben said as he opened his pocket watch and heard a locomotive pass along the tracks outside the border station. He stood and felt the glass cutter in his robe pocket. "How 'bout we find that train station now, brothers."

The End

Emil and Seren were survivors of concentration camps during the Second World War. They were in their early twenties then; both came from a small city in Hungary called Beregszász, located by the foothills of the Carpathian Mountains. Emil and Seren didn't know each other growing up, but their paths most likely crossed at least once. Those two people would eventually become my mother and father.

The character Benjamin Weiss is the protagonist in *Help of Angels*. He's based on my father, but unlike Benjamin, who ends up being taken out of the concentration camp and placed into the safekeeping of a Benedictine monastery, my father never had that good fortune. Ben's parents, Mendel and Hanni Weiss, portray my grandparents on my father's side, Adolph and Hanni Zeger. Mendel's five sons and three daughters represent my father's siblings.

I never had the opportunity of meeting my father's parents and three of his four brothers, but throughout the writing process, it seemed like we got acquainted by a kind of channeling, or psychic communication; I would visualize their bodies and faces, and listen while their voices spoke from the great beyond. The more I became immersed in the story, the more those relatives I never met, revealed themselves to me.

In the first chapter, Hanni Weiss, Benjamin's mother, is lighting two candles before the Friday sunset to commemorate the beginning of the Jewish Sabbath. The Weiss family sit at the dining room table and take part in the Sabbath evening meal. The blessings are said over the wine and bread, then Hanni and her three daughters serve bowls of hot chicken soup. Thirteen-year-old Benjamin Weiss will have his bar mitzvah the next morning.

If you sit down at your table and close your eyes, you might even imagine yourself at the Sabbath table with them.

While I was surfing the internet several years ago, by chance or otherwise, I discovered the names of my great-grandfather and great-grandmother on my father's side, Baruch, and Leah Zeger. They lived during the 1800s, in or near Beregszász. I don't have much information regarding my great grandparents, although I can tell you the name of one their sons, Adolph, my father's father. He was born around 1888. Baruch and Leah raised Adolph to be a *mensch* (a Yiddish word defined as a man of integrity and honor). Adolph Zeger had married Hanni (Chava) Rosen, and the small but strong woman eventually gave birth to three daughters and five sons: Ignatz, Arnon, Morris, Emil (who would later become my father), and Herschel, the youngest sibling in the family. They named their daughters Margaret, Serena, and Rosie.

Adolph Zeger earned a decent living in Beregszász by delivering packages from his horse-drawn wagon; an early-day Federal Express service, so to speak. Hanni, Adolph and their eight children acquired milk from a cow they kept in the backyard barn. Their eggs came from the chickens they raised. My grandfather wasn't a wealthy man, yet he had the means to feed his family, buy them new clothes for the Jewish holidays, and put a roof over their heads. That all came to a crashing halt one day.

In March of 1944, disaster struck the Jews living in Beregszász, and all over Hungary: German troops invaded the country. Elite Nazi soldiers trod up and down the main streets of Hungary's cities, shaming Jews by ordering them to wear the yellow Star of David on their outer garments. Next, the German and Hungarian armies forced Jewish residents out of their businesses and homes, transporting them to crowded, unsanitary, and inhumane detention centers, or ghettos. (The foreshadowing of the concentration camps.)

Between May and August of 1944, an alliance of German and Hungarian authorities arrested my father, his father and mother, his brother Herschel, sister Rosie, and approximately 3,600 of the remaining Jews in Beregszász, and they brought them to a brick factory on the outskirts of town. There, the displaced residents waited days or weeks for trains to deport them to various camps throughout Europe. During that time, my father, his parents, a brother, and a sister, along with thousands of other men, women, children, and infants were crammed into boxcars. The trains left Beregszász and towns and cities all over Hungary, en route to various concentration camps. My father woke up at a train station in Mauthausen, Austria, where he and the large group from Hungary were marched through the town, then imprisoned at the Mauthausen concentration camp.

My father's parents, his sister Rosie, and his brother Herschel disembarked the train once it stopped at the Auschwitz death camp in German-occupied Poland.

Along with hundreds from Hungary, the four of them walked onto the train platform, where they participated in a selection process supervised by Nazi medical doctors. The deportation trains continuously delivered thousands more terrified people into Auschwitz day and night. Many of them had suffocated inside the boxcars, long before they arrived at their final destination.

From the spring to the fall of 1944, over a hundred trains deported 401,000 Hungarian Jews to Auschwitz. Thousands more Hungarian Jews and Gentiles had been delivered to various other camps, while deportation trains from several other European countries brought millions more Jews and non-Jews as well. It's estimated that over 564,000 Hungarian Jews died between 1941 and 1945. From the 800,000 Jews who were living within Hungary's borders from 1941 to 1944, only about 255,500 were thought to have survived.

Adolph and Hanni Zeger were most likely murdered in the gas chambers, or by some other method the same day they set foot in Auschwitz. Their names are recorded in the "Hall of Records" at the Yad Vashem World Holocaust Remembrance Center in Jerusalem, Israel. There's no record of what happened to their youngest son, Herschel. He was either murdered the same day he arrived in Auschwitz, or died from some other cause at a later date inside the camp. A young woman, Rosie Zeger, was registered as a prisoner of Auschwitz. The Russian army liberated the camp on January 27, 1945. By then, approximately 1.1 million or more human beings had perished, Jewish and Gentile alike.

Seren, my mother, was hiding in Budapest, Hungary, when the Nazis arrested her. They put her on a train that was headed for Bergen Belsen, a notorious concentration camp once located in the northern part of Germany. An estimated 50,000 or more prisoners had been exterminated there, including the Dutch girl from Amsterdam, Anne Frank, who wrote the now famous book, *Diary of a Young Girl.* The British and Canadian armies liberated the camp on April 15th, 1945. When the Allied forces arrived, they found thousands of starved and diseased men, women, and children. Despite receiving immediate medical attention and food, many of those prisoners were in such ill health, they couldn't live past a few days. Another 13,000 corpses were scattered around the grounds; all were buried in mass graves.

My mother and the other survivors in her group hung onto life while a Swedish relief organization helped them out of Bergen Belsen. They were taken by ship to a Christian convent/hospital in Sweden, where nuns, nurses, and doctors spent weeks nursing the gaunt and sickly survivors back to health. I recall a photo album my mom kept at home, which contained shots taken of her and some other women recuperating inside the convent, shortly after they had left Bergen Belsen. It was soul-wrenching how my mother and the other women looked in those earlier photos, compared to the group photos taken of them months later, after they had convalesced, regained their health, and were ready to leave the convent. My mother briefly worked at a factory in Sweden before sailing on an ocean liner from Stockholm to America. The huge ship docked at Ellis Island, off the coast of New York City. Her first step in becoming a US citizen. My mother's Aunt Esther (her mother's sister), who once lived on the Grand Concourse in the Bronx, not far from the old Yankee stadium, had sponsored my mother to come live in America. She was taken under her aunt's wing, and she started a brand-new life.

By the 5th and 6th of May 1945, the United States Army liberated the main and sub-camps of Mauthausen. Close to 60,000 men, women, and children were freed. By the most amazing miracle, my father walked out of that God-awful hell alive.

My father once said to me, "The first thing I ate when I got out of the camp was a whole jar of mustard." I don't believe he ever ate mustard again. Another poignant thing he mentioned about the camp that chilled me to my bones: "The lice in the barracks ate us up alive."

After he was liberated from Mauthausen, Emil Zeger returned to his hometown of Beregszász, where he found the Russian army had confiscated his mother and father's house and property. He reunited with his only surviving brother, Morris, who had spent a length of time in a labor camp in the Russian province of Siberia. The orphaned brothers eventually left Beregszász and immigrated to America, where they joined their beloved sisters, Margaret, Serena, and Rosie, who had previously started a new life for themselves in Newburgh, New York (the city where George Washington, the first president of the United States, had his home and headquarters, which still overlooks the Hudson River).

In the early 1950s, a young and brave Emil and Seren, still unknown to one another, had been officially introduced by relatives in New York City. The man and woman from Beregszász, were married in a traditional Jewish wedding held in the Bronx. The couple settled in Newburgh, where they raised a family of two sons and one daughter.

My father had learned how to cut glass in Beregszász before he was deported. When he had arrived in Newburgh, he continued to learn his trade, eventually becoming a highly skilled glazier. In a relatively short amount of time, he would establish his own successful business, Emil Zeger Glass. A few years later, he and his brother opened the also lucrative Zeger Brothers Paint and Hardware store, that was once located on Broadway in downtown Newburgh. The two brothers worked hard, thrived, and made a decent living in the Hudson Valley.

After my Aunt Rosie was liberated from Auschwitz, she left Poland and immigrated to the United States, settling in Newburgh, close to her siblings. She met and married Ralph Monitz. They became my godparents when I was born. As a little boy, my mom and dad would take us to visit them. Aunt Rosie and Uncle Ralph once owned a simple white house on Henry Avenue, in a neighborhood known as the Heights, a part of town with a gorgeous view of the Hudson River, Mt. Beacon, and Storm King Mountain. West Point military academy is located farther to the south.

In my adolescence, I had attended seventh grade at South Junior High School in Newburgh, N.Y. The school is in the Heights, not far from where my Uncle Ralph and Aunt Rosie once lived. Sometimes, I would spend my school lunch break at their house. One afternoon, during one of those lunch breaks, my aunt and I were sitting in the kitchen that looked out onto their backyard. I glanced at the blue serial number that was tattooed on the inside of my aunt's forearm. I never had the courage to ask her about it before then; I did that day. At first, my aunt got mad, then extremely uncomfortable. She rapidly placed a hand, or a sleeve of a sweater over the embarrassing tattoo of numerals. She awkwardly explained, "I was given the numbers when I went inside the concentration camp." That was the first and the last time I spoke to my aunt regarding Auschwitz, or any other camp for that matter.

I'm certain my parents and relatives suffered greatly from what they had endured in the Holocaust. I could read it in their eyes, their auras. Those concentration camp memories surely must have haunted them terribly at times, as if they wanted to wake up from a dreadful nightmare but could not. For the life of me, I'll never fathom how my mother and father coped with their horrific past. My father discussed his time in Mauthausen to whomever would listen. My mother was just the opposite. I think she dealt with her phantom memories of Bergen Belsen—and what had happened to her there—by storing that deep, dark past far away; to a place she never wanted to revisit. I sensed her sadness; a sadness that reflected in the pools of her dark-brown eyes. My early exposure to the Holocaust inevitably depressed me. I was angry my parents and so many more people had to go through that hell. When I became a teenager, I wanted my mother and father to talk to someone about being in the camps and receive some sorely needed therapy. Whenever I asked my mother, she would only reply, *"I don't have a problem—I don't need to talk to anyone.* "It was basically the same story with my father. Denial is a terrible thing. I would eventually be the one to obtain psychotherapy regarding the Holocaust story. Writing this book was a deep-felt therapy for me.

Despite all that, my mother and father were triumphant, good, loving, and caring human beings. They remained strong after leaving Europe and wouldn't allow their traumatic past to defeat them. My parents never went back to Hungary; nor did they have a desire to.

For many years, I was bitter and angry about the Holocaust, along with the people who orchestrated it. I will never understand it, period. It's my feelings the Holocaust should never, ever be denied, cancelled, or erased from the world's history books. I pray there will *never again* be such a tragedy. I still struggle to forgive whoever was responsible for that genocide. I don't want to leave this world with hatred in my heart. I don't want to carry that horrible baggage to my next destination. (Forgiveness of such a large scale, is a work in progress.) I need to move forward with my life, without bitterness, without animosity in my heart. Perhaps if I try, I might even experience some joy in this wonderous life. It's a work in progress.

Each and every soul who comes to this planet, has an opportunity to discover for themselves: that love, respect and understanding for our fellow brothers and sisters, this precious life, the environment, the earth's creatures (no matter how big or small) may be the only path to follow. Everyone has the freedom to choose their own beliefs. You may ask, do I believe angels exist? Absolutely. I think there are billions of them. Maybe trillions. Everywhere. I believe that a higher power, a

Supreme Being, a God exists. So why wouldn't this Almighty Creator employ celestial beings in His great works? We might even be angels for all we know. Perhaps it's time we helped one another.

Glossary

Achtung: attention! in German

Arbeit macht frei: German for, work will set you free. The ironic motto that was displayed on the entrance gate to the Auschwitz concentration camp.

Ailes d'ange: French for 'Angel wings'

bimah: Hebrew for the podium, or platform where the ark in a synagogue is situated. Prayer services are led there, and the torah is read from.

bissel: a little or small amount. Yiddish

challah: a traditional braided bread baked for the Jewish Sabbath and holidays.

Chasid: a man of a strictly orthodox Jewish sect. Yiddish.

Danke schön: German, for thank you very much

Die Endlösung der Judenfrage: German meaning, "the final solution"

fater: Yiddish for father

Haftorah: one of the biblical selections from the Books of Prophets, read after the torah is read in the synagogue during the Saturday morning service.

Igen: Hungarian for the word yes

Juden: German for Jews, singular, Jude

kinder: German for children

Kübelwagen: A German light military vehicle used during WW2; it was the forerunner of the Volkswagen Beetle.

L'chaim: Yiddish interjection used in toasts, meaning "to life!"

Jawohl: German for the word yes

mazel tov: Yiddish word meaning 'good luck'

meshugana: Yiddish slang for someone who acts in an insane manner.

mezuzah: a piece of parchment called a klaf, which is contained in a decorative case and inscribed with specific Hebrew verses from the Torah. These verses consist of the Jewish prayer, Shema Yisrael, beginning with the phrase: "Hear, O Israel, the Lord our God, the Lord is One."

muter: Yiddish for mother

Nein: German word for No

Roux: is a French term for a mixture of fat (especially butter) and flour used in making sauces.

shul: A Yiddish word referring to a synagogue. Comes from the German schule, meaning school.

schnell: quick, in German

schlep: Yiddish for 'to carry a cumbersome load'

Schmutzig: German, for dirty or filthy

Schweinehund: A German insult defined as, pigdog

tateleh: Yiddish, for an obedient little boy

tallis/tallit: a prayer shawl worn by Jews in the synagogue

Tefillin, or phylacteries: A set of small black leather boxes and straps that contain scrolls of parchment inscribed with verses from the Torah. The tefillin are worn by observant Jewish men during weekday morning prayers said at home or in the synagogue

Wunderbar: German, for wonderful

yarmulke: a head covering worn by observant Jews. Also known as a skullcap or kippah.

Acknowledgements

Special thanks and gratitude to my editor, Liz Ferry. Much appreciation and thanks go out to Professor Winston Aarons, my former writing teacher, who taught me a lot about fiction from his writing classes at The Old School Square in Delray Beach FL. Thank you Dimitri, Sheri, Barbara, Petra, Mary, and Kathy for your generous help with ideas, grammar, story and plot development. And most importantly—your love, wisdom, and laughter.

Do not fear the terrors of the night

nor the arrows that fly in the day.

Dread not the thief who lurks in darkness

nor the catastrophe that strikes at midday.

Although a thousand may fall at your side

and ten thousand perish around you,

these atrocities can't harm you.

See how the wicked are chastised.

If you make the Lord your home and refuge,

no bad influences will overpower you.

Just realize the wicked are punished.

No disease will affect you.

For He will order his protecting angels,

everywhere you travel.

Psalms 91 verses 5-11

Made in United States
Orlando, FL
25 October 2022

23838676R00176